RHAPSODY AND REBELLION

ONCE UPON A WIDOW #2

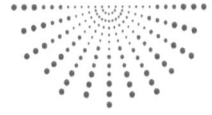

AUBREY WYNNE

RHAPSODY AND REBELLION

BY AUBREY WYNNE

Once upon a widow©

A Scottish legacy... A political rebellion... Two hearts destined to meet...

Raised in his father's image, the Earl of Stanfeld is practical and disciplined. There are no gray lines interrupting the Gideon's black and white world. Until his mother has a dream and begs to return to her Highland home.

Alisabeth was betrothed from the cradle. At seventeen, she marries her best friend and finds happiness if not passion. In less than a year, a political rebellion makes her a widow. The handsome English earl arrives a month later and rouses her desire and a terrible guilt.

Crossing the border into Scotland, Gideon finds his predictable world turned upside down. Folklore, legend, and political unrest intertwine with an unexpected attraction to a feisty Highland beauty. When the earl learns of an English plot to stir the Scots into rebellion, he must choose his country or save the clan and the woman who stirs his soul.

COPYRIGHT

ISBN: 978-1-946560-14-8
Editing by The Editing Hall
Proofing by Paula Proofer
Cover by Sweet N Spicy Designs

To my readers: where would I be without you? Thank you for always inspiring me to write one more.

PRAISE FOR ONCE UPON A WIDOW SERIES

Praise for *Once Upon a Widow* series:

"Historically accurate with poignant characters dealing with strife so gut-wrenching, I can't even imagine how I'd respond. Gripping story with an explosive ending."

N.N. Light Book Heaven Reviews

"Aubrey Wynne's epic historical romance bedazzles as much as it leaves the reader breathless! Her intricate details lavish the reader with picturesque landscapes, scrumptious dialogue, leaving nothing too small to define."

InD'tale Magazine

"Somewhere between Austin and Heyer. A good read."

Amazon review

"The scenes are so graphically detailed and descriptive, it paints an elegant backdrop that makes the storyline pop."

"This well-written piece has a balance of sorrow and happiness it will make you cry, smile, and maybe even jump with joy. I highly recommend this charmer."

"Aubrey wields her words as skillfully and precise as a surgeon with his scalpel."

"I highly recommend."

"Another author for my favorite list."

FOREWARD

Rhapsody and Rebellion is #3 in the Once Upon a Widow series.

This book was originally a part of The Enduring Legacy series. Each book told the stories of the descendants of one family that were persecuted during the height of the witch trials in Scotland. This family is not real, and is the work of fiction, but what happens to them very much occurred to individuals in the sixteenth century and beyond.

The special legacies are handed down to the MacNaughtons through three siblings from 1590 Scotland and include the gift of sight, the gift of empathy, and the ability to see the Truth. They are persecuted because of their gifts and desire to help others. However, their children are saved and their legacy continues to live on.

In Rhapsody and Rebellion, Gideon learns he has inherited the legacy of Truth while his mother has secretly possessed the gift of sight.

PROLOGUE

ONCE UPON A WINDOW©

"Rebellion against tyrants is obedience to God."

— BENJAMIN FRANKLIN

June 4, 1792
King's Birthday Riots
Edinburgh, Scotland

*T*he noise outside grew steadily louder until Maeve's mother, Peigi, snapped the drapes closed. Specks of dust danced in the slivers of sunlight, beckoning Maeve to investigate the muffled cries for justice, the shatter of glass, and splintering wood outside the window. The bedlam on the city streets was horrifying and riveting. It reminded her of the first time she'd witnessed a deer hunt, not wanting to watch the dying animal but unable to look away.

A sheen of sweat covered Ma's face in the humid, still air of the dining room. Maeve reached out and squeezed her fingers in reassurance. "He'll be here soon."

They would be safe with Da. He was bigger and stronger and more astute than anyone she'd known in her fifteen years. The sound of horseshoes and carriage wheels crunched in the driveway. A moment later, the heavy oak door slammed open. Calum MacNaughton filled the doorway, wild black curls clinging to his neck and strong jaws, a whip in his hand.

"Let's go, my lovelies. We dinna know how long this uproar may last." Sapphire blue eyes glittered with urgency. "I've rented a hack to get us out of the city limits. The carriage is too tempting for the rabble."

Maeve picked up her heavy skirts with one hand, grasped her reticule with the other, and hurried for the door. The footman tossed baggage on top of the hansom then returned to assist Maeve. Her heart beat rapidly as she settled on the worn padded bench. A far cry from the soft velvet of their own carriage. Maeve had been delighted to accompany her parents to Edinburgh. Now she prayed for the safety of her Highland home.

"What if they stop the carriage? I'm frightened, Calum." Panic added a shrill pitch to her mother's voice.

"They're just hungry and tired of not being heard. I willna let any harm come to ye." Her father's calm tone soothed both the women. "Now up ye go, Peigi, my love. We'll be out of here in the blink of an eye."

He sat across from them, rapped his knuckles against the roof, and the vehicle lurched forward. The horses whinnied in protest and sidestepped men running through the streets and debris flying in their path. Someone tried to hitch a ride on the side of the vehicle. Calum swore under his breath, leaned out the window, and punched the man in the face. The trespasser fell on his arse in the mud, waving an angry fist and holding his nose.

The driver headed toward a narrow alley to avoid the throng of rioters. Maeve peeked out the window to view the square, packed with hundreds of people streaming in from all sides. On a shoddily erected platform hung a noose, with a group of workers balancing what looked like a man on their shoulders. They tied the noose around his neck. One of his arms swayed unnaturally by his side, and she sighed with relief when bits of straw fell from the coat sleeve.

The coachman cracked his whip, careened into the alley, and broke free of the crowd. As the noise subsided, Maeve listened to her parents argue about the political situation that had led to the insurrection. She leaned her head against the hard bench, each rut jerking her neck back and forth. It had been such a long day, with little sleep the previous night. Her lids grew heavy, and she gave in to a fitful sleep.

The horde of men jeered and poked flaming torches at the driver and team of horses. Their clothes were filthy, and they had an air of men used to taking what they needed. A man of wealth poked his head out of the gleaming carriage, his tall hat hitting the window frame and toppling to the dusty ground.

"What are you hooligans about?" he demanded. "I order you to step aside and let us cross the bridge."

One of the men laughed, his yellow teeth protruding from his cold smile. He appeared to be the leader. "Sorry, milord, but we canna do that. In fact, we think it's time you traveled the same as the rest of us."

"Look here, I insist—"

Two of the rabble pulled the nobleman from his upholstered seat and sent him sprawling across the dirt road. The stiff breeze picked up the clouds of dirt that swirled into little grayish brown whirlpools. Another man touched his torch to the wooden bridge in several places. Embers glowed then spread, crackling as the flames began to lick at the dry planks.

"Looks like ye won't be crossing the stream today, unless ye don't mind getting those Hessians mucked up." The group laughed as the leader picked up the hat and placed it on his own head.

"You will all pay for this. Do not think this attack will go unpunished."

"I beg yer pardon, my lord, but this topper here could feed my family for a month or more. Can't imagine yer family ever goin' hungry."

"And to be honest, the riots in Edinburgh are keepin' the constables a bit busy."

The earl rose and brushed himself off, only to be cuffed in the jaw and sent back to the dirt. Just as he managed to rise onto all fours, a kick in the gut sent him down again, clutching at his belly and moaning with pain.

A shot rang out. One of the rogues crumpled to the ground. The driver stood, a shaky hand still pointing a smoking pistol.

"Well now, that wasna verra polite." The leader removed his newly acquired hat, set it carefully on the dead man, and rolled up his sleeves. "I'm afraid I'll have to teach ye a lesson in manners before ye have time to reload that thing."

A blade flashed and landed in the driver's chest with a thump. The earl cried out as his cravat was yanked from his throat then wrapped around his neck once again. His well-manicured fingers dug at the makeshift noose. His face turned purple, a gurgling, hacking noise escaped his gaping mouth, and his body slowly slumped to the ground.

"NO!" Maeve sucked in a breath and sat up.

"What is it, daughter?" Her mother brushed back an

auburn lock that stuck to her cheek. "Ye've slept like a restless spirit on Samhain."

"We canna take this road. There are highwaymen ahead who have set upon travelers and torched the bridge."

"Hush, now," Ma soothed. "It was just a dream. I'm not surprised with the day we've had."

"No, ye must listen. They've murdered a nobleman and his driver." She squeezed her eyes shut and rubbed her temples, trying to bring back the image and push away the throbbing pain in her head. "It's too late to help them, but we shall be the next victims if we continue on this route."

Calum pounded on the roof and stuck his head out the window. The coach came to a halt, and he left the women inside while he spoke with the driver. "Now tell me exactly what happened in this dream," he said, once again settled across from them.

An hour later, they stopped outside a small copse of trees. Behind them, smoke rose into the air. The driver yelled from above, "A sound idea to take a lesser traveled road, sir. It looks like the bridge is on fire. Must be thieves making trouble. The rabble like to take advantage in times of unrest. I don't think we'd enjoy making their acquaintance." With a crack of the whip, the carriage lurched forward.

Her mother exchanged a troubled glance with Da. Then he leaned forward and cupped her chin in his fingers. His soft voice belied the concern in his deep blue eyes. "Have ye had these visions in the past?"

Maeve nodded, her bottom lip trembling. "When the barn burned, I dreamt of it the night before."

"Ye've inherited the family legacy, lass. One of the abilities passed down for centuries in times of trouble."

"*One* of the abilities?" She shuddered, wondering what other secrets were hidden in their past.

"Your grandmother had the gift of empathy, which made

her a natural healer. It came in handy with wee ones or unconscious patients who couldna tell what ailed them. She also spoke of a third ability to see the truth in a man's soul. We never ken when a child will be born with such powers."

Maeve shook her head. "But I don't *want* this legacy. Why me?"

"The visions only come when there is a chance to change an outcome, to protect the future of our clan. As you have just done." He rested his elbows on his knees and clasped her hands in his. "It's an honor and a heavy burden. And I wish to all the saints that I could save ye from both."

CHAPTER ONE

ONCE UPON A WIDOW©

"Those who dream by day are cognizant of many things which escape those who dream only by night."

— EDGAR ALLEN POE

August 16, 1819
Stanfeld Estate,
County of Norfolk, England

Gideon touched the horse's flank with his boot, moving into a smooth, rocking canter as he focused on the distant stone wall. His muscular body moved with the gelding, his thighs gripping the saddle, and his hands resting lightly on the reins. Still in training, Verity had been worth every pound. He had heart and courage and would gallop over a cliff if asked.

Marked as a rogue and a bone-setter at Tattersall's

auction, the horse had apparently refused to bend under training or listen to the whip. But the gelding's eyes had held intelligence when Gideon stroked his wavy dark forelock and blew gently on his nose. The "beast" turned out to have more common sense than most of those roughriders, who thought to break an animal's spirit with fear and domination. The three-year-old wanted to please but had rebelled against unwarranted pain. The fading scars that marked the ebony hide from sharp spurs and countless lashes proved it had not been the proper incentive. Verity enjoyed a challenge and learned quickly when asked with kindness. Animals weren't much different from people really, except perhaps more trustworthy.

The pair approached the hedgerow. Gideon leaned forward and grabbed a fistful of mane with his spur hand. A subtle cue and the horse sailed over the shrub, landing grace-fully on the other side. The wind pulled at the opening in his shirt, and it billowed around him with a flapping noise. He gave Verity a pat on the neck and eased him into a trot. "Good boy!"

The cool morning breeze lifted the hair off Gideon's neck and cooled the sweat running down his back. The sweet smell of fresh-cut hay filled the air and he breathed deeply. His eyes swept over the green pastures and dotted hills that had claimed his imagination as a child. Playing with the village children and fighting dragons on ancient ponies, looking for buried treasure, or going to war against the Danes or the French—depending on the most recent history lesson. Where had that adventurous youth gone?

Verity's ears pricked forward. Gideon chuckled at the scruffy little brown mutt bounding up the hill. "Good morn to you, Little Bit."

The dog barked in reply, his tail wagging so rapidly that it seemed a blur. "A race, you say?" Little Bit barked his agreement. "I'll tell you what. I'll keep him in a trot to make it fair."

The threesome ambled west, their backs to the sun. They crested a hill and the sight of his childhood home in the distance, standing sentry over the countryside, filled Gideon with pride. The numerous windows of the imposing three-story medieval manor glinted and flashed like jewels in a crown of gray sandstone. On each corner, gable, and the entrance sat miniature turrets like arrows pointing to the heavens. Surrounded by the original moat, it reminded visitors of long-gone knights, fair maidens, and chivalry. A wide, arched bridge spanned the ditch, bricks matching the color of the mansion and providing ample entrance to the estate grounds. Rolling hills and grazing pastures surrounded the mansion on three sides with acres of forest along the back. From atop this hill, it was an impressive sight, and Gideon always enjoyed watching people's reaction the first time they saw it.

Little Bit barked, tail wagging and feet pawing at his stirrup. "My father passed on quite a legacy, didn't he? Now it's up to me to maintain and improve it."

He leaned down to give the dog a final scratch then headed down the hill at an easy canter, mentally ticking off the correspondence he would respond to after breakfast. The estate's steward also wanted to update him on some newly acquired livestock. There was the appointment with the solicitor next week in London concerning the textile mill in Glasgow. The business had been his father's personal project so Gideon was eager to learn more about the details of that particular investment. It was the only corner of the Stanfeld holdings the late earl had seen to himself.

London. The visit would be a two-edged sword. On one hand, he looked forward to a few nights of gaming and camaraderie with good friends. Perhaps a stop at Tattersall's to see what was on the auction block. On the other hand, those voracious, title-seeking mothers with their simpering single daughters… At least the families were sparser this time of year. At twenty-five, he still enjoyed his bachelor status and tried to avoid the town in the spring and early summer as carefully as horse piles on a busy street.

Just before crossing the bridge, he dismounted. Little Bit rushed ahead, barking a warning that his master was home. Gideon paused beneath one of the yew trees flanking the bridge, tucked his shirt into his breeches, and rolled down his sleeves. The reddish brown bark shown with purple in the morning light, and the low hanging branches swayed softly in the breeze. He walked across the bridge, buttoning his cuffs, his boot heels clicking against the bricks. The water below sparkled as lilies floated lazily along, an occasional fish making a splash. A stable hand waited on the steps, holding a crust of bread out to the dog.

"Give him a long rubdown. He worked hard this morning." Gideon gave the horse another pat on its muscular neck and handed over the reins.

"Yes, my lord." The man led the animal away, the tatty pup at his heels.

Sanders, the butler, greeted him at the door. "Good day, my lord. Lady Stanfeld is waiting for you." His gray eyes, matching his thinning hair, danced with humor as he collected his lord's waistcoat, crop, and gloves. "She appears to be making a list."

Gideon groaned. "Of females?"

"Yes, my lord, I'm afraid so."

"Thank you, Sanders." Gideon ignored the family portraits and the suit of armor stoically standing guard as he strode through the entryway. Intent on changing before greeting his mother, he bounded up the circular staircase two steps at a time.

Gideon entered his chambers, finished a quick half-bath, and wiped dry with a clean linen towel. He dressed in fresh buckskin breeches, a white cambric shirt, a brandy-colored waistcoat, and finished tying his cravat as he hurried down the stairs.

"Good morning, dear Mama," he murmured as he bent low to kiss her cheek. "You look fetching in that deep shade of lavender. I'm happy to see you finally out of those blacks. It doesn't suit you."

"I've followed the English tradition of mourning in honor of your father. But I'm happy to have some color back. It brightens the skin." Her words still held the barest hint of a Scottish accent. Maeve smoothed her crepe skirt and smiled. "I've been waiting for you."

"So I've been told. Perhaps some coffee before you bombard me with your list?" Gideon smirked at her surprised look until those dark blue eyes flashed with determination. He held up a hand. "I'll listen with interest as soon as I've finished a cup and had something to eat."

Maeve watched in bemused silence as a servant poured the steaming black liquid into a china cup. Gideon lathered soft butter onto a thick slice of fresh bread and scooped some cherry preserves on top. With a groan of delight, he chewed with his eyes closed and finished with a smack of his lips. "This season's cherries were superb."

Maeve opened her mouth then closed it as he reached for his coffee. She made a face.

"And is that displeasure aimed at me, Mama?"

She shook her head. "I don't know how you can prefer that horrible drink to tea. And without even a drop of milk or lump of sugar."

He grinned, spearing a piece of cold beef with his fork. "I

have my father's dour demeanor and prefer the bitter to the sweet. Now, who is on your marriage agenda?"

She frowned. "It is not an agenda or about marriage. I've decided to have a small dinner party, and I've listed a few names that might be of interest."

The last thing Gideon wanted was to be surrounded by tiresome young ladies looking for a husband. But seeing the light back in his mother's eyes, he kept his thoughts to himself. It had been over a year since she had accepted an invitation or entertained. He was willing to be the sacrificial lamb to see her reenter society.

"I am happy to play host for whatever event you would like to arrange. Now about that list…"

His mind wandered as she told him of the families that would receive an invitation. His father had endured these social affairs as a matter of course. Always the proper gentleman, always the mannered aristocrat, always the impassive Englishman. Life was a set of rules and one followed those tenets to the letter in private, in social circles, and in business. The world, according to the late earl, was black and white.

The exception had been his wife, the vibrant and outspoken Maeve of the prominent Clan MacNaughton. The earl had disliked the superstitious and rebellious Highlanders but had fallen in love with one of the chieftain's daughters. She had seemed to be the only weakness in his inflexible world, the only person or thing he allowed to let him stray from society's rigid rules. Gideon had seen her pull caps with him and hold her own, occasionally even winning an argument. Those instances had ended with a wicked glint in his father's eyes and a smug smile on his mother's lips. Then the two of them would hide away in their bedchamber the rest of the day.

"I received a letter from Marietta last week. She'd like to

visit before winter. So I will plan it as a welcome dinner in September. She's finally with child, you know. It may be quite some time before she can travel again."

The last words sounded wistful and brought Gideon back to the conversation. Marietta, the eldest sister, was less than two years behind him. Then came Charlotte, four years his junior, and Helen the youngest at eighteen. All had married well, in their father's opinion, with the exception of Helen. She had wed a wealthy base-born Irishman. "It will be good to see Etta again. I'm surprised Lord Burnham is allowing her out of his sight. After three years, I swear the man is still smelling of April and May."

"There is nothing wrong with being in love. And he'll most certainly keep a close eye on that girl." Maeve laughed. "She's still a bit impetuous, but motherhood will slow her down."

"I hope something does." He rose from the table and kissed Maeve again on the cheek. "I will leave you to your preparations, then. I'll be with the steward for the rest of the day. "

***

The accounts for the quarter completed, Gideon and Jethro Birks admired the sheep littering the grassy hillside. They were fine stock and his steward had finagled an excellent price the previous year. "Outstanding job. I'm impressed with the results of the spring shearing. Damn good wool and damn good profits."

"It took some talking, my lord, but I finally convinced your father to let me bring in these sheep from Gower. Much better quality than the Vale long wool and brings twice the price." The summer sun had bleached Jethro's hair almost white, making his brown eyes and tanned skin appear even darker. He pointed in the direction of a southern pasture. "I'd like to try grazing the cattle same as the sheep.

Get the animals out of the yards, and we'll see better milk and beef."

"With your past record, I'm inclined to trust your judgment on this. By god, you even managed a second hay cutting this summer. There'll be plenty of feed for the winter."

"Can't take all the credit for that, my lord. The weather helped a bit."

Gideon looked over the acreage with a contented smile, his father's words coming to mind. *Surround yourself with competent men, treat them well, and your land and finances will prosper.*

This was proof of that philosophy. He'd known Jethro since they were boys, hunting squirrel with slingshots and swimming in the horse pond. He was the third generation of Birks to manage the Stanfeld estates, and Gideon was thankful to have such a downy steward.

"I'll be in London for a few days, checking in with the solicitor. Fair warning"—he cleared his throat—"Lady Stanfeld has come out of mourning and is planning a country party for September. What she has described as a small dinner gathering will no doubt turn into a week of company."

"Yes, my lord. Consider me prepared for the upcoming requests."

"Give my regards to your charming wife." Gideon turned his gelding back toward the manor. It had been a productive day, and he was ready for a glass of sherry and a good meal.

***

The Countess of Stanfeld settled into her favorite chair near the library hearth. She held a small book of poems and read a few pages until her eyes grew weary. Her thoughts strayed to her late husband Charles and the heart condition that had sapped his strength his last years. It had made him weak of body but not weak of mind. He had remained lucid and pragmatic until the end, knowing death was upon him and looking the reaper in the eye. Maeve had always admired his supreme will and saw that same strength in her children.

But he had also been a narrow-minded man in a sense, whose rational views did not allow him to see anything except what lay in front of him. If it was not factual or quantifiable, it was not real. He had laughed at her first vision of a sinking ship he planned to invest in, indulging her recount as if it were an amusing story. Until it came true. It had shaken the very foundation of everything he considered Truth. Rather than look too deeply into the situation, he shunned the unexplainable. Ran from it as if it were the devil himself after his soul.

His reaction had been swift and irrevocable. Her female mind was too easily swayed by homeland folklore. Maeve would not return to the Highlands while there was breath left in him. She would remain in England, become a proper countess, and forget the mystical nonsense of her childhood. By that time, she loved him so deeply that the fear in his eyes had frightened her also. He didn't understand, didn't have the capability to conceive of something so intangible, other than God. And he struggled with that omniscient presence. So she never told him of another vision, and instead did what she could to avoid tragedy whenever possible. She willingly gave up her childhood home for him but refused to give up her family.

The earl had compromised with his wife and in-laws by going to the Scottish Lowlands and meeting in Glasgow twice a year. The couple had first been introduced in that city, when Charles and her father, Calum MacNaughton, had met to discuss the purchase of a textile mill. Her father still insisted the papers had only been signed after Maeve had agreed to his courtship. The trips satisfied the desire for her children to know the MacNaughton clan. Gideon had always been especially close to his grandfather, growing more like his image every year with Calum's muscular build, black hair, and piercing blue eyes.

She smiled, closed her eyes, and gave in to a pleasant afternoon nap.

He pushed against the throng of men, women, and children to hear the gentleman on the stage. The stink of unwashed bodies and a hum of excitement filled the air. He pulled off his waistcoat as the sweat pooled beneath his collar. The speaker's words of reform and the right to vote echoed in his head and filled him with purpose.

A woman holding a small child sidled up next to him, a smile on her lips. The pair made him think of his own wife and the family they would have. The wee girl had the same dimples as her mother. The babe waved a hand at him, and he caught her chubby fingers in his. Grasping her mother's braid in her other hand, the babe sucked heartily then began to cry as the noise increased. She squealed as the crowd jostled the pair and reached toward him. The pressure of bodies behind them intensified, and the hair on the back of his neck rose. Something wasna right.

Screams pierced the air, and he turned to see the cause of such panic. Mounted Hussars stormed the assembly, the rhythmic whisk of blades slicing the air. A glistening black beast, eyes rolling, lunged forward then reared. Flying hooves pawed at the scrambling bodies and struck the infant in the head. The mother screamed, her arms reaching for the falling child.

He pushed the frantic woman away from the soldier's sword then threw himself on the tiny, lifeless form. "Ye bloody bastards," he cried as the horse reared once again.

This time its full weight landed on his back. The crack of bone echoed in his ears. Excruciating pain exploded along the length of his body. From the ground, he saw a jumble of feet and hooves, all moving in different directions. A man's face—contorted in pain—trampled by the frantic feet escaping the massacre. He tried to hunch over the child still beneath him, protect it from the stampede, but his body had been flattened. An image flashed of the local butcher pounding a tough piece of meat.

A blow to his head...a piercing throb... Then the world spun in slow motion. The shrieks of victims and harsh shouts of the soldiers came from far away now. Another image. His sweet wife's face.

"I'm so verra sorry, Lissie..." he whispered.

***

Gideon entered the library, still warm from the afternoon sun. Mama sat before the fireplace, the large wingback almost swallowing up her small frame. She had aged in the last year. A few streaks of gray now blended with the rich auburn hair. Her eyes were closed, but her lids fluttered as if dreaming. The sapphire ring, a wedding gift from her husband that matched her eyes, glinted and winked as her slender fingers gripped and released the armchair. Her head rocked back and forth as Gideon squatted down next to her. His fingers covered hers, and he squeezed to wake her from such troubled sleep. The touch sent a jolt through her body. Her eyes snapped open.

"No!" she gasped, her gaze fixed on the darkened hearth.

"Mama, you were dreaming." His thumb stroked the top of her hand, his voice soft and soothing. "Look at me, Mama, and you will see."

Maeve slowly turned her head, tears now spilling down her cheeks. "Oh Gideon, it was ghastly."

"What did you dream?"

"It was not a dream." Her voice faltered. "Your cousin, Ian, is dead."

"What? Did you receive a letter from Scotland?" Gideon had not seen any correspondence from his mother's family over the last week, and nothing had arrived today.

"I do not need a letter. I saw it. There's been a terrible slaughter in Manchester, and Ian was trampled..." She lifted her chin and wiped at her wet cheeks with determination. "You must take me home to my clan."

"To the Highlands? You haven't been there since your wedding." He sighed and rubbed the back of his neck. "I can't just run off to Scotland with my aging mother because of a dream."

"Aging?" Her eyes narrowed, anger shining from beneath her lashes. "I have more stamina than most of those mutton-headed females of the *ton*."

He had to agree with her but bit back a smile. "This is folly. A trick of the mind from lack of sleep." He pressed his lips to her fingers. "Let's have a glass of sherry, and you'll feel better after we eat."

"Don't patronize me. Your father didn't believe in..." She took his face in both her hands, strength growing in her touch and her gaze steady and direct. "It doesn't matter. Listen to me. It was not a dream but a message of sorts that we are needed at home."

"This is our home." Gideon stood and leaned an arm against the fireplace mantel, worried the past year had also taken a toll on her mind. An uprising in Manchester? There had been rumblings throughout parts of the country but nothing significant.

"This is *your* home. *Mine* has always been in Scotland, regardless of how long I've been away." Her eyes pleaded with him.

"What about Marietta's visit in September?" That would end this foolishness, he was sure.

"It will have to wait until October. You must promise we will leave as soon as you return from London. Or I will go alone."

He looked up to the ceiling, hoping for some divine intervention. None came. "I give you my word."

CHAPTER TWO

---

*"Un-thread the rude eye of rebellion, and welcome home again
discarded faith."*

— WILLIAM SHAKESPEARE

August 1819
MacNaughton Castle
Scottish Highlands

*A*lisabeth was lost without him. Utterly adrift among the clan members she'd always considered a second family. She had been betrothed to Ian for as long as she could remember. Her family was part of the smaller neighboring clan of Craigg, who pledged fealty to the MacNaughtons. She and Ian had grown up together, played and fought together in the hills and heather, and swam together in the nearby loch. The two clans had celebrated every solstice and Samhain at MacNaughton Castle.

As part of a long ago agreement to mend the clans, the Craigg had offered his first granddaughter in marriage to the MacNaughton's firstborn grandson. Though after her grandfather's death, her parents had given her a choice once she'd been of an age. But she had known the marriage was her destiny from the bond shared since they were children. So Alisabeth had happily said her vows at the age of seventeen. A year later, she floundered in a sea of sympathy, struggling to accept his violent death and grasping at the wisps of her future. Who was she, if not Ian's intended?

A few of the Glasgow weavers, who had traveled with Ian to Manchester, had wrapped him in linen and carried his body back across the border. The men had considered it an honor and their duty to bring home Calum MacNaughton's grandson. He was a respected chieftain, and the weavers were all either members of his clan or lived in nearby Dunderave. It had been two days since Ian's corpse had been laid out, and Alisabeth could not bear one more word of condolence or look of pity from the constant stream of well-wishers. A continuous flow of ale and food, provided for those family members and close friends keeping watch over his still form, had resulted in numerous ghostly tales and stories of remembrance. Her husband, always so full of life, would have loved hearing the humorous recounts and correcting their exaggerations.

"Ye need to eat something, Lissie," said Ian's grandmother, Peigi, over the boisterous laughter coming from the dining hall. One thick gray braid hung down her back, matching the black and silver stripes of the fine wool arisaid that extended from her shoulders and past her slight hips. She wrapped an arm around Alisabeth's shoulders, her faded green eyes filled with concern. The other hand absently rubbed the circular silver and garnet clasp that held the long shawl in place. "My grandson would be angry if I let ye waste away."

"I had a biscuit this morning."

"Och, ye canna survive on a bit of bread. Think of the bairn ye may be carrying."

Alisabeth shook her head, picking at the embroidered band around her waist. The intertwining crimson circles on the belt provided the only color on her black linen skirt and bodice. Tears threatened to spill down her face, and her voice was barely audible. "No, my menses came this morning."

"Shh, Lissie, shh. I know it's a disappointment. For all of us." Peigi set the bottles down she had gathered for the guests.

"Lass, stop torturing yerself over things ye cannot control." Another burst of deep laughter floated from the other room. "Let's be more like our men folk and think of the good times. Ian would want us laughing with the others, not off by ourselves crying on what might have been."

If Alisabeth had been with child, the MacNaughtons would have been her family until she died. But as a widow with no bairns, she would most likely go home. The emptiness in her heart consumed her. Although she and Ian had not been a love match, he had been her closest and most trusted friend since she could remember. Their relationship may not have been passionate but their deep affection and fierce loyalty to one another had given them a more solid foundation than most couples ever achieved in a lifetime of living together.

"Let's join our neighbors, shall we?" The old woman wrapped her in a fierce hug. Her soft, wrinkled cheek touched the young wet one, sharing the tears.

Alisabeth nodded. Her mother saw them enter and moved forward. She tenderly adjusted the white kertch covering her daughter's hair and smoothed it down her back. "How's my Lissie?"

"Fine until I see yer eyes go all soft, and then mine begin

to burn." She sniffed and gave her ma a watery smile. "How does a mother manage to bring out those emotions her children always try to hide?"

"It's maternal instinct, and ye'll have it one day. I promise." She squeezed Lissie's hand. "Now, is everything ready for tomorrow?"

"Aye." After the funeral, she would find a quiet place to curl up and mourn. And decide what to do next. Go home? Who would she share her dreams with? Who would laugh at her clumsiness? Who would understand her better than Ian had? She needed to escape the benevolent looks and find a new purpose. It would give her comfort in the days to come.

A few days later, the MacNaughtons gathered in the outer court to say goodbye to the men from Glasgow. They had used the funeral to take a holiday from the mill and spend time with their families. The first rays slanted over the stone towers, shimmering off the trees and creating a dance of silver and shadow against the old castle walls. The weavers mounted their horses and tipped their hats. Colin, the senior tradesman, spoke for the group. "Our sympathies, to the family and especially to ye, as the widow. Ian was a fine man. Times are troubled, and he was someone we could count on. Our worries are not over, and we dinna know what the future brings. A man of yer husband's stature and understanding will be sorely missed."

"We are in yer debt for bringing his body home to us. I canna imagine my grandson buried on English soil." Calum held out his hand to each man.

Alisabeth saw the pain in the men's eyes. Ian had been a more than a supervisor. The weavers were known for being a close-knit group and his death left a broken chink in their armor. "I understand ye are hoping for representation in the English parliament. My husband was verra passionate on that subject. I wish ye luck."

"We appreciate that." He nodded to the south. "Now we best get moving. Looks like we'll come across a bit of weather on our way home."

As they spurred their horses, she put a hand out and ran after Colin. He pulled back on the reins and halted. With a racing heart, she blurted, "I may only be his widow, but I'd like to honor his passing. If there is ever anything I can do to help yer cause, ye need only ask."

The men nodded and murmured their thanks. Colin leaned down and squeezed her shoulder. Silver lightened his dark hair at the temples, but his clear blue eyes held strength and did not reflect his age. "I will keep that in mind, lass. We thank ye kindly for the offer."

Her thoughts went back to her last conversation with Ian.

"Why are ye insisting on finding a new overlooker for the weaving factory?" Lissie kneaded the dough, pummeling it with her fists to relieve the tension in her neck. "Let the new Lord Stanfeld find a replacement."

"Mo chridhe, have we not had this conversation? The long trips take a toll on Granda though he's loath to admit it. Hasn't had his heart in it since the old earl became bedridden, and Auntie Maeve quit the visits to Glasgow." Ian tipped her chin up with a finger. "So he's passed the duties of the family business on to his grandsons. It's time for Gideon and me to pick up the reins now for the clan."

She nodded. "Do ye not think yer cousin will want more of a say?"

"Nay, an English earl wouldna dirty his hands with trade. Our families share the profits from our weaving factory with that understanding. Without his investments, the MacNaughtons wouldna have the business." He ran a hand through his unruly red

waves. "We have a responsibility to see that it's run properly. It supports not only our clan but half the village."

She snorted and pummeled the dough again, making him laugh.

"I'm glad that's not my face." He poked her in the side. "Besides, I want to take a trip to Manchester and see the weaving machines they have. Twice the production, they say. And I'll get a better price on supplies."

"Don't give me excuses. I know ye too well. Ye want to hear that Henry Hunt speak." She wiped some flour off her forehead with her sleeve. "I fear for yer safety when ye are with those radical workers."

"We are a passive group, Lissie. No harm will come to us. The Patriotic Union in Manchester is proclaiming a peaceful assembly, and it's been approved by the magistrate."

Alisabeth sighed, tossed the dough into a pan, and covered it with a cloth. "And ye trust those Englishmen?" Looking up into green eyes always sparkling with humor, she gave in and smiled back. She would not part ways with angry words between them. "Fine then, off ye go. And look for a pair of long silk gloves to match my green dress, please."

"Only if ye promise to stop doing chores in the kitchen. It pains Ma to see ye working like a servant."

"Och, it's not like I'm toiling over the fire or washing the cooking pots. Baking soothes my nerves." She grinned. "And it's better than punching someone when I'm angry."

"Aye, and less painful too. One black eye from ye was enough." He pulled her braid. "I was only seven but a man doesna forget such an insult."

Alisabeth smiled at the recollection of that black eye. So many memories, so many happy times... She burrowed her hands inside the deep pockets of her skirt, caressing the silk gloves that had returned with Ian's body. Life was so precious, and she had taken her joy for granted. Never again.

***

The funeral was over and most of the long distance guests finally gone. Those remaining, including Ian's siblings and Alisabeth's parents, had retired to their quarters above. She began picking up cups and plates, helping the housemaid to keep her hands busy and her mind blank. The empty dining room seemed unnaturally quiet after the last few days.

"We'll move to the sitting room," announced Peigi as she and Calum paused in the doorway. "It's more comfortable and private for our own reminiscing."

The three of them took the narrow stone stairs up to the second floor, where her bedchamber and several others were also located. The smaller room had been paneled and the floor covered with gleaming wood planks. It was filled with personal items rather than ancestral paintings or antiques. Miniature portraits framed in silver or delicately carved wood sat on the mantel. A large bible sat on a side table next to Calum's chair, its leather cover faded and the binding worn from constant use. Peigi often read from it in the evenings at her husband's request.

An oak table with four matching chairs sat at the far end of the room, an ivory chess set ready for a match. Its polished pieces had seen dozens of games won and lost on a rainy day or winter's evening. Thick wool rugs of red, gray, and cream, scattered about in front of furniture and the fireplace, provided a warm haven for bare or stocking feet.

Alisabeth paused at the door, realizing she might not be here this winter to enjoy the crackling fire and camaraderie of the MacNaughtons. She would never again sit on the chaise longue next to Ian, lay her head on his shoulder, and sing a ballad or listen to the haunting chords of the small pipes or fiddle.

"Bring me my tobacco, lass," Calum called to her. "And pour us all a swallow or two of sherry."

She smiled at that phrase. A swallow or two often led to an entire decanter. Perhaps the liquor would dispel the chill inside her.

"Ye are welcome to stay here, lass." Calum whispered in her ear as she leaned over to hand him the leather pouch. "But if ye wish to go home when yer family leaves, we will understand."

She had been thankful for her parents these last few days. But her mother's sympathy had been almost suffocating. To go back with them, and be enveloped in their well-meaning pity, seemed a worse fate than her grief. Craigg Manor no longer seemed her home. She had been a child there and grown into a woman here. It would be like stepping back in time. Yet remaining at MacNaughton Castle, she would forever be haunted by thoughts of Ian. How would she move on?

"I thank ye, Calum. The MacNaughtons have always been verra good to me."

"Glynis may need ye for a while longer. She isna ready to let go of her son yet, and ye will give her comfort."

"We give each other solace." Alisabeth's voice cracked as she poured three glasses of the amber liquid. Sharing her mother-in-law's sorrow was preferable to enduring her family's sympathy for now. "I'll stay as long as I am needed."

Calum squeezed her hand. "Ye'll be provided for as long as ye are a widow, whether ye stay or go. Not to worry."

She nodded, the lump in her throat blocking any response. The past few days had been long and difficult. But the nights were worse. The description of Ian's death would replay in her mind as soon she closed her eyes. The mangled body that had returned, the description of his death—and others—had been gruesome. The men had spared no details. The nightmares returned every evening when her tired mind finally slept.

"Da! Da, I've a letter from Maeve." Ian's ma came running into the room, waving an envelope. She broke the wax seal and unfolded the parchment. A hand ran through her thick auburn waves as her eyes scanned the thick vellum. She began to read.

My dearest Glynis,

There are no words to heal a mother's broken heart. I will not try to write empty condolences. Instead I am coming home. I want to wrap my arms around my sister, feel her sorrow, and let it fall upon my own shoulders. We will cry together and then begin the mending. I will miss the funeral but shall be there in spirit. God keep the MacNaughtons safe until I arrive.

With all my love,

Maeve

Glynis sank into a chair and covered her face with her hands. Alisabeth gently removed the letter from her grasp as the tears fell.

"It will be good for yer soul to see Maeve again. It's been three years since our last visit to Glasgow and almost thirty years since she's returned to her home." Peigi sat next to her daughter, stroking her hair.

"Stanfeld wasn't up to the travel those last few years. And she wouldna leave his side."

"She willna be breaking her promise." Glynis sniffed. "She told me she couldna return to the Highlands while he still had breath. Now the man is dead, she is free."

"Hush, love. Her husband dinna understand us, but he was a good man. His money provided us the opportunity to prosper. And prosper we have." Peigi hugged her youngest daughter. "Maeve is coming home. Let us celebrate what we can in this dark time, hmm?"

The family all nodded in agreement. The tick of the clock and an occasional sniffle from Glynis were the only sounds for several moments.

"I wonder if she will bring my grandson? He looked more like me each summer." Calum took his pipe from the small table beside him. He leaned over and tapped it against the hearth, the cold ashes spilling into the burning peat embers. Settling back into his stuffed wingback chair, he filled the bowl with tobacco. "And has he inherited anything else from the MacNaughtons?"

Peigi and Calum's gaze met and held. Their expressions were sober, as if they shared some long ago secret. A thread of worry needled down Alisabeth's spine. Why did she have a feeling this visit was more than what it seemed?

CHAPTER THREE

"Truth is always strange, stranger than fiction."

— LORD BYRON

Late August, 1819
London, England

"*D*amnation!" cursed the Viscount Pendleton as the last card sprang up from the small taro machine. "I've lost enough for one night."

Gideon laughed at Nathaniel. He had joined his long-time friend at White's. It was his last night in London, and he wanted to relax a bit and catch up on any personal or political news. "You realize this is nothing but a sham, an amusement of chance? You could just as easily toss that pile at a willing wench and get more for your coin. Stick with those games that use strategy and employ a player's abilities and shrewd observational skills."

"So sayeth the ever-rational Earl of Stanfeld. I agree, but you must admit I tend to be a deuced lucky corinthian."

"Not tonight."

"And you, my friend, always seem to do well when you're in the mood to play. In fact, I can't ever remember you losing. It's almost as if you can see your opponents' cards."

"Nonsense, I'm just an excellent judge of character and have a sense whether a man is bluffing." He slapped Nathaniel on the back. "What do you say we go collect a decanter of the finest brandy and gamble on who's left standing at the end of the night?"

Pendleton chuckled. "I remember the days when I might have easily lost that wager too."

"And I don't think your Eliza would appreciate a sodden husband at this particular time." Gideon clapped him on the back. "I hear congratulations are in order."

The viscount grinned. "As if I don't have my hands full already with that precocious three year old. But at least Althea's given me practice for my firstborn. She has a ridiculous amount of energy and lack of attention."

The widowed Lady Eliza had a daughter from her previous marriage. Gideon wondered if he would have been as generous and able to accept another man's child.

"I haven't dealt with many children, but I do believe most of them are on the wiggly side." He wondered what his sister Etta's child would be like.

They settled into chairs in front of a bow window while Gideon ordered refreshments. As they waited, they remarked on the carriages driving past or pedestrians they recognized —mostly male—on their way to another gaming hell or gentlemen's club on St. James. A tray arrived with two crystal snifters and a decanter of golden liquor.

"Terrible shame up in Manchester, eh?" Pendleton asked once the brandy was poured.

"Manchester?" Apprehension stirred in his belly.

"The riot. Parliament started this mess, too busy keeping their own pockets filled and ignoring the political unrest. The merchants are calling for equal representation in cities like Manchester. But those same merchants won't provide fair wages for the skilled artisans or factory workers. The tariffs on grain imports have kept the prices high, which benefits the landowners, but the masses need to eat.

"Too many taxes and the lower classes take the brunt of it," agreed Gideon.

Pendleton threw back his glass of brandy. "A peaceful crowd at a gathering to listen to a speech on passive reform —women and children were there, mind you. The bloody Tories will drive the working class from reform to revolt if they don't keep their paranoia under control."

Gideon's stomach clenched. "Tell me more, I'm not sure I heard the entire story." To his shock, he *had* heard most of it. A few days earlier in his own library. As Pendleton recalled the facts, a pounding began in his head. His mother's dream had been uncomfortably accurate. But how?

"I read the details in the Times just this morning. Calling it the Peterloo Massacre since it happened at St. Peter's Fields. At least twenty dead and hundreds injured. I'm sure infection will take more and increase the death toll," concluded Pendleton.

Lost in his thoughts, battling a now queasy stomach, Gideon missed the rest of the summary. Then a fresh brandy was put in his hand.

"So Stanfeld, what is this I hear about you going to Scotland?"

Gideon pulled his mind from the confusing web now clouding his brain. He'd figure it out later. There *had* to be an explanation. "My mother is insisting she returns home for a month. Since I need to inspect the mill in Glasgow, I've decided to extend the trip to MacNaughton Castle."

"The Highlands, then?" Pendleton whistled then held a hand to his ear. "I can hear your father through Heaven's Gate, scratching your name in his black books."

"It's the least I can do for Mama after this past year of mourning. And as I said, I have business across the border anyway."

"My wife's mother was a Scot. Quite a beauty at one time." Pendleton's lips turned up in amusement. "Perhaps you'll find a diamond of the first water hiding in the heather."

Without thought, Gideon pulled at his cravat, happy to be on another subject. "That's my mother's hope. She's started a list."

His friend groaned in sympathy. "I've been there, my friend. My condolences."

"Yet you are happily married. So perhaps the institution's reputation has been exaggerated."

"That all depends on the woman. Take Eliza, for example." Pendleton leaned forward as if warming to his favorite subject. "The sweetest of temperaments but the heart of a warrior when it comes to protecting the defenseless. It's how I met her, you know. She can make me laugh one moment and boil my blood in the next.

"In other words, the right female may be worth the parson's trap, but each one brings her own peril to the party."

"Exactly!"

***

Mid September

Gideon pulled the collar tightly around his neck. Water poured off his hat, down his back, and dripped off his nose. The rain had been unrelenting since they'd left the inn that morning. He hated being imprisoned in the carriage, but he was close to giving in. The greatcoat gained weight with each mile, and his shoulders were beginning to ache. They had made Edinburgh two days ago and would reach his grandfather's home before the end of the day. He hated this part of the country already. Soggy, dreary, and those blasted thistles. At least the road was holding out—there was so much rock that the mud hadn't been a problem yet.

With a resigned sigh, he hailed the driver and the wheels sloshed to a stop. He dismounted, tied Verity to the back of the carriage with the spare horse, unbuttoned his capes, and shook them out as he opened the door.

"I knew if I was patient, the rain would eventually drive ye inside. We need to talk."

Maeve smiled with a smugness that irritated him. He carefully removed his hat and dumped the contents of the rim outside. When he slammed the door shut, the wooden window slats rattled. He *had* been avoiding this conversation. However, he needed an explanation before they reached MacNaughton Castle.

"I agree. Shall I begin?"

She nodded her consent and pulled a handkerchief from her reticule. "Dry yerself and speak up. This storm is verra loud upon the roof. Has the other carriage caught up with us yet?"

"Almost. Your maid does not seem to enjoy the travel as much as her mistress. She looked half terrified when I informed her you preferred to travel alone today." He wiped off his face and neck then ran the cloth over his head. "Now, let's start with your speech. The closer you get to Dunderave, the thicker your brogue becomes." Had this been true during their visits to Glasgow? He didn't recall. But then again, the Lowlanders didn't speak the Gaelic as the Highlanders did.

"It's in my blood, Gideon. I suppose the more I'm exposed to my kinfolk and clan members, the more I hear it on their tongues... To be truthful, I hadn't noticed. And I won't apologize for it or try to hide it." Her chin jutted out in that familiar way that silently told him she would not give in to this point.

"It was only a question, Mama. It matters not if you say 'don't know' or *dinna ken*. But I would like to know if Father required you to speak as an Englishwoman." He had begun to suspect his mother's life in England had not been easy.

His parents had loved each other, yes, but the late earl had been inflexible in his opinions and stringent with societal rules. What had she gone through as a young girl of eighteen in a foreign country, surrounded by strangers who looked down on her bloodlines and upbringing? He was sure the *ton* would have presented their false smiles then turned their noses up as soon as the Earl of Stanfeld turned his back. His mother was perceptive and would have known she was seen as an outsider. Yet somehow, she had won their respect and even made valuable friendships.

Maeve sighed. "Aye, he hired a tutor to help me with my diction. It pleased him, and I enjoyed learning the cant. The lessons helped fill the hours with your father gone for days at a time. Then I made friends, had children, and needed no other diversion."

Gideon nodded and decided to get to the point. "How did you know about the rebellion? I'm not calling your dream a *hum*, but I can't credit you as some sort of gypsy fortune teller who can predict our future."

"Then you explain it to *me*, please. You said yourself that ye didna hear about the Manchester trouble until the solicitor mentioned it in London. The Times reported the entire event so it's not gossip." Her hands were gripped tightly in her lap, fingers entwined, knuckles white. Her voice caught. "And your cousin is dead, leaving a young widow barely married a year."

His hand swiped over his face, jaw clenched. He prayed for patience. Again. "Perhaps someone on the estate heard rumors, and you overheard a conversation without realizing it." He held up a hand when she opened her mouth. "We know Ian had taken over the mill for Grandfather and went to Manchester on occasion. *Perhaps* these pieces floated about in your mind and came together in a dream."

"*Perhaps,*" she mimicked.

The sun chose that moment to appear, sending bright rays poking through the blinds. Maeve pulled the satin rope and was presented with a view of narrow ridges interspersed with sharp peaks, capped with white and dotted with green. Shadows played light then dark, rolling over the landscape and making the mountains appear alive. She gave a satisfied sigh and leaned back against the cushions, a smile on her lips. Gideon thought she looked years younger.

"Your father may have molded you into his image, Gideon, but half my blood runs through your veins. Now that you have bestowed me with your suppositions, may I tell you what is certain?"

He ground his teeth but moved his mouth up in an attempted smile. "Of course."

"I have a gift, or a curse, depending how one sees a legacy such as this. Since I was a girl, I've had dreams that come true. When Da realized it, he explained they were visions, an ability passed down through our family over the centuries. It often skips generations but appears when needed. I only have these dreams when there is a possibility of changing fate's course." She paused. "This is why I needed to come home."

"But Ian is dead. How did your dream help him? It didn't alter history or save the lives of those at St. Peter's Field." He shook his head. "This makes no sense."

"Then the vision wasn't meant to save Ian or the others

but someone else. It is yet to be realized." Her voice was quiet but steady, no pleading for understanding in her tone, no anger at his speculation. Just a steadfastness that proved she spoke the truth. Or believed she did. They sat in silence for some time.

"So we will spend a month in the Highlands, hoping to unravel the mystery and our role in changing the course of history?" He kneaded his forehead with the ball of his palm, wondering what calamities lay in store.

Maeve leaned across the carriage and squeezed his hand. "It will take time for you to accept my visions. I pray I never have another. Och, you may never accept my visions *or* your own ability. Only time will tell."

"*My* ability—"

"There it is." His mother pushed her entire head out the window and pointed to a tower in the distance. "I hadn't realized how much I missed it until now."

When she sat back down, her eyes glistened, a trembling smile on her mouth. He'd never seen her look so lovely. "I will leave you to a private homecoming. It is time for me to return to the saddle." With a smile, he kissed her cheek. "I'll reassure your lady's maid we are close to our destination."

The next two hours passed quickly. With the rain gone and his clothes only damp, the Highlands spread out before him like an illustration in a book. The hills seemed to pile one upon another, sometimes poking through clouds, while mist crept around and between the hollows. Below, the deep valleys were lush with clear, fast-running streams running along their bottom. Much to his surprise, Gideon found the terrain rugged but beautiful in its stark simplicity. The land beckoned him, drew him in, and he had the urge to spur Verity into a gallop and explore what was in the nearby copse or over the next ridge.

Gideon had been ready to dislike this country, and he had

at first. But now its essence seemed to swirl around him, gently pushing him to notice the vibrant contrasting colors, the earthy smell of rich soil and pungent pine, the chatter of red squirrels, and screech of golden eagles or peregrine falcons. It was a landscape that stood proud in its history, not apologizing for its irregularities or unpredictable weather. His mother had been shaped by her birthplace.

"Gideon! Gideon look," Maeve called from the carriage, pointing to the narrow winding path ahead. "We're almost there."

He urged Verity back and rode alongside the carriage as they made their way up the incline, listening to his mother explain about this crumbling structure or that decaying wall. A rectangular stone keep stood above them, a round tower built into its far north corner, overlooking the countryside. The edifice loomed over a courtyard and a group of people waving and shouting. Two Scottish deerhounds lounged beneath a rowan tree, letting out an occasional bark. They were not close enough to discern faces or hear words but Gideon grinned. He'd recognize his grandfather's tall, dark form from any distance. His grandmother would be clucking and calling their names.

A deep longing swept over him, an inexplicable need to belong to these people. As the voices grew louder, and his name could be heard in the excited prattle, he found himself happy to have come. It must have shown on his face.

"You dinna regret the trip," his mother said cheerfully as wheels crunched the gravel and slowed to a stop. "I'm glad."

He barely had time to dismount before the MacNaughtons descended upon them with hugs and tears and slaps on the back. He and his mother didn't have time to answer one question before another was asked.

"How were the roads?"

"Did ye catch any rain?"

"Ye must be parched."

A shrill whistle pierced the air and silence descended. Calum looked smug as he withdrew his fingers from his mouth. "My daughter and grandson need to catch their breath and refresh themselves before we ambush them like a pack of wolves."

A murmur of agreement, a brief hush, and the cacophony began again. A chuckle grew and spilled out of Gideon, joined by Calum. "I see nothing has changed."

"Och, lad, why would ye want that?" He nodded toward the keep door. "Welcome to our humble abode. It's not much to look at these days, but it's belonged to our clan since the fourteenth century."

MacNaughton Castle was everything he expected of an ancient keep. Outside, the thick walls dominated the architecture with narrow slits for light on the lower floors and larger windows above. Compared to the elegance of Stanfeld Manor, MacNaughton Castle was unembellished and solid. It reminded him of Calum MacNaughton. He loved it.

A bell clanged and a woman called from the entrance. "Refreshments are served."

His gaze locked on the most exquisite girl. Her hair was dark but not black. More of a burnt umber. A white scarf covered her head, but it did nothing to contain the thick waves that fell around her small waist and rounded hips. Honey-brown eyes watched him curiously, and a shy smile curved her full pink lips. She wore mourning clothes but rather than dim her beauty, the dark color enhanced her creamy skin. The word enchanting sprang to his mind.

A servant? A local villager's daughter? Such a striking girl —she did appear young—added to the castle's charm. Gideon had a sudden urge to know more about her. A local beauty could certainly help pass the time.

CHAPTER FOUR

"Fear not for the future, weep not for the past."

— PERCY BYSSHE SHELLEY

"Thank ye, Lissie." Calum turned to the group. "Ye heard the lass, inside with the lot of ye."

They stepped into the dark entryway and proceeded into a large receiving room. Taking the narrow stairs to the first floor, their heels clicked on the ancient stones and the women's skirts rustled against the steps as they ascended to the dining room. The table had been set with warm bread, cheese, smoked salmon, fresh berries, and stewed apples.

"We thought ye may be hungry after yer journey," said the young woman, Lissie. "Would ye like tea, ale, or wine?"

Gideon could not take his eyes off her. Her husky voice settled over him, followed by a wave of heat. He changed his mind. She was gentle bred not a serving girl or kitchen maid.

He pulled out a chair for his mother and grandmother. Peigi patted the seat next to her.

"Please an old woman and sit yer handsome face here."

Calum guffawed and took his place at the head of the table. The two hounds, one a sandy red and the other a dark blue-gray, lay at his feet, one on each side. The darker one lifted its head as his master absently scratched his shaggy rough coat. "Gideon could be me forty years ago. I imagine that rankled Charles a wee bit." He pulled out a chair for Aunt Glynis and Lissie. So his second guess was correct.

"He preferred to think I took after *his* mother's family. And Mama indulged him," Gideon added as he studied the room. While the outside had been left to the elements, inside the castle had been renovated with paneling, large rugs, and painted ceilings. The wealth was evident in tasteful antiques or sculptures placed on shelves or tables. The platters and silver shone with polished care, and the smell of fresh baked goods tickled his nose. For all the cold gray on the outside, the tower house was inviting and comfortable.

"I must apologize to ye for my lack of manners. This is my daughter-in-law," said his aunt. "This is Alisabeth, Ian's wife...widow..." She sighed as her eyes closed for a brief moment then smiled. "She's been my saving grace these past weeks. I dinna ken what I'd do without her."

The woman blushed and lowered her eyes. "We've been a great comfort to each other."

Disappointment then guilt surged in his chest as Gideon realized this stunning creature had been his cousin's wife. She was grief-stricken, and he was concentrating on that delectable mouth. *Good god, man,* he thought. *My apologies, Ian, I didn't know.*

"It's a pleasure to meet you. May I offer my sincere condolences?"

The sadness in those amber eyes pierced his soul. She was so young to experience such a burden. He searched for words that might ease her sorrow but was at a loss. Instead he said what was in his heart. "Ian was a fine man, and he will be greatly missed."

Her gaze fell upon him and he had the urge to stroke her cheek and tell her all would be well. "Please, we dinna stand on ceremony here. Call me Alisabeth or Lissie. And I thank ye for the kind words."

Their eyes met and held, and then she smiled. Warmth rushed through his body again—or God forbid, was it a blush? This time satisfaction filled him instead of regret.

He'd pleased her and it made him glad.

***

Alisabeth stood at the door, unable to interrupt the intimate family reunion. If Ian had been alive, he'd have pulled her into the gathering. But he was not. She recognized Lady Stanfeld as she stepped from the carriage, the same deep blue eyes as Glynis and Calum, the striking auburn hair Peigi once had, and the smile that marked every MacNaughton. As the voices rose, she slipped back into the castle and made sure the refreshments were set out.

The kitchen had sent up fresh bread, cheese, and baked apples. The scent of sugar and cinnamon filled the hall. She took a deep breath, feeling the confidence seep back into her bones as she issued orders and fell into a familiar role. Satisfied all was in order, she returned to the courtyard.

Alisabeth heard a whistle as she reached the door. In the fleeting silence, a man straightened, and her heart stopped. A lock of coal black hair fell across his forehead, and he pushed it back with long fingers. Below a straight nose and high cheek bones, flexed a strong jaw. His waistcoat stretched across his broad chest and shoulders. Tan breeches hugged muscled thighs and calves that disappeared into mud-spattered leather boots. A foreign heat spread through her limbs, and she grabbed the bell rope used to call the children, and pulled until it clanged.

"Refreshments are served."

Vivid sapphire eyes locked with hers and knocked the breath from her lungs. Embarrassment warmed her skin, but she did not look away from his handsome face or try to stop the small smile forming on her lips. Her stomach fluttered as it had when she was a child, jumping from the high rocks into the loch. As the group moved into the cool dim interior, Alisabeth could smell his spicy scent. Orange mixed with salt, probably from his sweat during the long ride. It created a unique musky smell that tickled her senses as Lord Stanfeld passed by her.

She could see the dust in the lines of his neck and fisted her hands, so she didn't reach up to wipe away the grime and brush the hair from under his collar. With a slight trembling, she wiped the perspiration from her palms onto her skirt. *Saints and sinners,* she scolded herself. *Stop fussin' over yer husband's cousin.*

Yet her body did not listen. When Glynis introduced them, his rich baritone sent a pleasant shiver down her spine. His genuine words about Ian warmed her and were appreciated. Such conflicting reactions made Alisabeth want to run from the room. Jump on her mare, race through the fields, and hide in her private spot by the water where she could sort through the confusion that filled her head.

"Once I am rested," Lady Stanfeld was saying to Glynis, "I'd like to take a walk and see what has changed."

"Not much, I warn ye. The stables have expanded with living quarters above." Aunt Glynis winked at Gideon and teased her older sister. "Do ye still ride or have the years caught up with ye?"

"I'll race ye to the glen, dear sister. Let me pick out a

horse, and we'll take a gallop this week. Gideon, are ye interested?"

"Do I have to race or can I follow behind and watch?"

"Suit yerself. But the loser will forfeit their shortbread Lissie is making for Sunday." Glynis frowned. "Maybe ye can convince her to stay out of the kitchens."

Calum held up his hand. "Not until she makes the shortbread. I tell ye, lad,"—he nodded at his grandson—"a scoop of fresh strawberry preserves on one of those biscuits, and ye'll be in heaven. Or mighty close."

"You cook?"

Alisabeth blushed when Lord Stanfeld gave her his full attention. It was odd to have the notice of another male that was not somehow related. "I bake bread, pies, biscuits and such. Ian and Calum enjoy their sweets, and the baking soothes my soul when my worries catch up with me. If only it soothed Enid's soul when I took over her kitchen. I thought she'd run me out with a broom when I prepared the dough for today."

"A cook would run you out of your own kitchen? I wouldn't allow staff to be so high in the instep."

"Our social class system isna recognized in the same fashion as in England. For example, when we have a *cèilidh*, which I'm certain we will," Lady Stanfeld said, looking pointedly at her father, "all the villagers and anyone working on the grounds will be invited."

Alisabeth watched his expression go from shock to curiosity to amusement.

"So there's no standing on ceremony when it comes to a party. What about marriage?"

"That's a wee bit different. Rather than titles, we tend to associate a good match with a clan." Calum smiled affectionately at her. "Lissie here was part of an agreement between my father and her grandfather during troubled times between our clans. The two chieftains decided that if our grandchildren were betrothed, it would keep the peace for at least five generations."

She felt his gaze and gave him a sideways look. His mouth was open. Closed. Open. Closed again with a snort. He didn't seem the type who would be at a loss for words, and she stifled a giggle.

"Are the daughters of titled men allowed to choose their own husbands then?" she asked. "I didna think arranged marriages were so rare in England, my lord."

He had recovered and now studied her with interest. "Most girls do as their fathers command. They have a choice within certain boundaries. It is more about an appropriate match than love, of course. My sisters, for example, would not marry a man without title or money. They can choose a prospective husband and as long as his bloodlines, and in some cases his bank account, are acceptable then all is well."

"The rule of thumb, they say, is marry up but never down." Lady Stanfeld shook her head. "One of the few rules Charles ignored because he chose me."

"I take offense to that, daughter. He moved up in my estimation when he asked for your hand."

"And that is all that matters, Da." She covered one side of her mouth and whispered loudly across the table. "Then there is my youngest, Helen, who ran off with the Irish bastard of a duke."

Alisabeth gasped, warming to the countess. She had a feeling they could be fast friends. "What did your husband do?"

"Ranted and raved and threatened to disown her. He even came up with a plan to sail to Ireland, kidnap her, and keep her hostage until she saw reason."

"What changed his mind?"

"Reminding him that Da could have done the same to me,

and it wouldna have mattered." Lady Stanfeld stood and walked over to place a kiss on Calum's cheek. "I am done to a cow's thumb. A nap is in order if I am to stay awake through supper this evening."

Glynis called for the housemaid. "Davonna, Lord and Lady Stanfeld are ready to be shown to their rooms. Please inform her lady's maid and have one of the girls start the water for their baths. I'm sure they'll need to wash a layer or two of dust off."

"Do ye ken what would make me truly happy?" the countess asked her sister. "Let me borrow some of yer clothes. These English gowns are pretty but much too thin for our weather. I've forgotten how chilled one can get in the mountains, even at the end of the summer."

The MacNaughtons beamed collectively, and Alisabeth realized this was the countess' way of letting them know she still respected the Highland ways. Glynis spoke first, a catch in her voice, "I've kept yer plaid and I'll bring ye a few skirts and bodices along with it after yer nap."

Lord Stanfeld rose and bowed. "I cannot express what a pleasure it is to finally be here. I am looking forward to learning more about the place where my mother grew up."

They left the room and no one spoke until the echo of footsteps faded. "Well Lissie, what did ye think of our Maeve and her son?"

She swallowed, wondering what Calum would say if he knew what thoughts she'd pushed from her mind. Stalling, she fed the dogs bits of crust while she searched for the correct words. "The countess is bonny and kind and truly one of ye, no matter where she's lived these past thirty years. And her son…"

"My grandson is a damn Englishman who needs to be reminded of his better half." He considered her a long while. "And we have verra little time to do it."

. . .

***

Gideon hung his shirt, waistcoat, and breeches across a chair and stepped into the tub. A fire blazed and he wondered again at the chill so early in autumn. What would it be like in the winter?

He let out a soft groan of contentment as the hot water seeped into his tired muscles. Leaning his head back and closing his eyes, the image of Alisabeth's face greeted him. She was a rare beauty. And the marriage had been arranged. Had she loved him? Had Ian loved her? He knew without doubt she mourned his loss, could read that easily. Still, there must be some special bond between her and the MacNaughtons since she was still here. Unless… Good God, he was a codpole. It made perfect sense. She was with child.

He cursed softly. The attraction to her had been immediate and unusual. It hadn't been just a physical desire that flooded him but something more… She was a conundrum, and he'd always liked puzzles. He'd figure it out—figure her out. Alisabeth, no he preferred Lissie, would be an easily solved mystery.

His mother, on the other hand, was a bit more complicated. The transformation already was remarkable. The joy in her expression, the softening of the deep lines that had appeared around her eyes and mouth over the last year, the energy that had returned to her body and spirit. Yes, this would be a rejuvenating trip for Mama. The doctor could not have prescribed a better antidote.

The water had cooled and he reluctantly stood, reaching for the pitchers on the floor to rinse his hair and body. He'd left the towel by the chair and walked across the braided rug, leaving a trail of small puddles behind him. As he wiped himself off, he peered out the windows. Below, Lissie collected herbs from the back garden. Those two hounds now sprawled under an elder tree, watching her as she moved through the rows. He recognized sage and larkspur as she added the former to her basket, bending to give him a view of her handsome backside.

A small boy with bouncing red curls skidded into the garden, causing the dogs to bark and thump their long shaggy tails. Lissie wagged a finger at him in warning, he supposed. It didn't work. The child threw his arms around her legs, sending the basket into the air. She struggled to catch it, lost her balance, and went sprawling into a patch of chamomile. The young boy threw himself on top of her, squealing with delight and inviting the dogs to join in the fray. Her hands covered her face then her stomach as she tried to protect herself first from canine kisses and then from small tickling fingers.

"Brownie, Angus, sit." The muffled words floated through the closed window. "Gavin, off me now, ye little banshee."

Much to his surprise, the dogs obeyed though their tails continued to thump, and Brownie, the female, began to howl. The young boy, Gavin, rolled off his mistress and reached out a small grubby hand to help her up. She said something to him, which made him grin, and they both retrieved the herbs that had spilled from the woven basket. Lissie tousled the boy's hair then froze. Slowly, she raised her head and their eyes met.

Her tawny orbs were bright even from this distance. He smiled, hoping she didn't think he was eavesdropping. Her eyes grew wide. Concerned, Gideon pushed open one leaded pane to ask if there was a problem. The fresh air hit his bare chest and he froze. *Tarnation!* Horrified, he looked down at the droplets clinging to his dark chest hair and clenched the towel in his fingers. The windowsill covered his lower half but only began at the hips. When he looked back toward the garden, Lissie was herding the boy and the dogs along the path. Before she disappeared around the elder tree, she peeked over her shoulder and gave him a mischievous grin. He grinned back.

The alluring Alisabeth: baker, gardener, caretaker of dogs and hooligan children, widow. She'd stoked his curiosity. Did she stay out of duty to the chieftan and the possibility of carrying an heir? Or did she long to be with her own kin but forced to remain here because of the unborn child? Gideon knew Ian was to inherit a portion of the MacNaughton lands and a share in the mill. The girl would be swimming in lard if it were a boy. Otherwise, it would go to his cousins Lachlan and Brodie. Yet he didn't get the impression that wealth was important to her. He'd get to know her better before he made a sound judgment. But if Lissie was as guileless as she was enchanting, he would make sure she was taken care even if she had a daughter.

CHAPTER FIVE

"I have been a selfish being all my life, in practice, though not in principle."

— JANE AUSTEN

---

*G*ideon donned a clean white shirt, gold waistcoat, and dark brown riding jacket with matching breeches and gleaming black boots. Combing his hair straight back then parting it on the side, he checked his reflection in the mirror. A shave would be nice but he didn't want to take the time before breakfast. Many of the men had beards so a little growth on his jaws wouldn't be out of place. It was a bit rebellious, he thought sheepishly. Only his third day in Scotland and already he was shucking English convention.

Like his father, he'd always been fastidious with his appearance. *A man must demand respect from the very first glance, or it will be an uphill battle,* the late earl had repri-

manded when he'd found his young son in a slovenly state.
Yet it was a different way of life here. Even his clothes made
him stand out in this part of the country.

The men wore the short or belted plaid in the
MacNaughton colors of red, dark green, and blue. Calum
had tried to get one on Gideon but embarrassment
prevented him. Nothing but a linen shirt beneath the yards
of material! He couldn't bring himself to bare his knees.
Then there was the complicated task of donning it. He'd
end up wrapped like an Egyptian mummy instead of
resembling a Highlander. The ridiculous reticule at the
waist also didn't appeal to him. Yet everyone seemed to
accept his presence, despite his mother's warnings that
Highlanders had long memories and many still did not
trust the English.

Today he would accompany his grandfather into
Dunderave and issue the invitation for the upcoming cèilidh.
It struck him odd that his grandfather didn't send a repre-
sentative to do such a menial chore. But his mother wanted
to go, so perhaps they had decided to make a day of it.

He entered the dining room and stopped, scanning the
room for Alisabeth. She had not come to supper the first
night. Not that he blamed her after his window display.
Yesterday she had been scarce, tending to the blacksmith's
wife, who was having a child. Why on earth they didn't have
a midwife or physician was beyond his comprehension.

The deerhounds sniffed at his feet. He held out his hand
when he found the female's soft brown eyes looking at him.
For the first time, she licked him.

"Aye, there's good a girl," crooned Calum. "She's beginning to trust ye. They're like us, ye ken, and need time."

Gideon looked sideways at the larger gray male. He held
out his hand, palm up. Angus curled a lip, his hazel eyes
narrowed. "Some of us need more time than others."

"Give him a bite of this, and he'll come 'round soon enough."

The smoky voice quickened his pulse as his eyes drifted over Lissie. A plaid shawl gave color to her black clothes, draped over her shoulders with a circular clasp attaching it at the chest. In the center of the silver pin was an engraved tower, representing the original MacNaughton Castle. Her thick dark waves were swept up in a loose bun, tendrils curling against her slender neck. She picked up a rasher from the sideboard and brought it to him. "No male can resist the smell of fried pork in the morning."

He laughed, took the thin slice of meat, and heard his stomach growl.

"And ye are no exception." She giggled and walked back to the array of food. Over her shoulder, she added, "Squat down and place it on your palm, or ye'll lose at least one finger."

He followed her advice, determined not to let a demmed dog intimidate him. The ham worked. Angus poked his head forward and sniffed at his palm several times then snatched the meat. When Gideon proceeded to the sideboard, the hound followed him.

"Now ye have a friend for life," said Glynis from the polished oak table.

He turned to greet his aunt but words escaped him. Next to her sat his mother, dressed in a similar fashion as her sister. Both in mourning colors made from a wool and linen blend, Aunt Glynis's skirt was black with a deep blue bodice, his mother's brown with a dark violet bodice. Mama's hair was pulled back in a tight knot, no curls or jewelry adorning her face or crown. She looked like a housemaid rather than the Countess of Stanfeld.

"Ye don't approve?" His mother chuckled. "Perhaps I should have warned ye, but I'm enjoying the shock on your face. I wish I could sketch your expression right now."

"I-er…" He avoided her gaze and filled his plate with rasher and eggs, beans and black pudding, and scooped some porridge into a bowl. His father had hated the blood sausage and "Scottish mush," but these were two breakfast items Maeve had insisted on every morning. He heard more scratching in Father's black books as he registered his son's full plate and his wife's dress.

"Weel, are ye ready to meet the local folk?" asked Peigi. "It will be a long day, mind ye. Perhaps ye'd like to ride yer horse in case the visiting gets a bit long. There will be several families that willna let Maeve go without a chat."

He bent and gave his mother a kiss on her cheek before seating himself across the table. He considered the possibility as Alisabeth watched him with interest. Perhaps… "Is anyone else riding? I prefer my mount to a carriage but hate to ride alone on a family trip."

"I wouldna mind. It's such a lovely day and winter will be here soon," Alisabeth offered. "If ye dinna mind the company. Calum often saddles up too."

"Now I'm torn between sitting with these beautiful lasses or enjoying a fine conversation with my grandson and Lissie." He scratched Angus's ear while he studied Lissie's hopeful face with a half smile. "If I ride, I can take the hounds. The exercise will be good for them."

"It's settled then," said Gideon, the morning already brightening. "How long is the journey?"

"Only an hour or so by wagon," answered Glynis. "But we're taking the long way to show you some of the country."

"And more than a few stories along the way, if I ken my da," added his mother.

Calum chuckled. "Why are we wasting time at the table then?" He cupped his hands around his mouth and yelled. "Archibald, send word to get the carriage hooked up. Gavin, tell yer nanna in the kitchen we'll be needin' the basket in an

53

hour. And dinna forget the mutton pies left over from last night's supper."

Gideon hid his amusement as he wondered how his butler Sanders would react to the master yelling orders across the hall. Probably die from apoplexy.

The older women returned to their rooms, discussing this family or another. Peigi mentioned a name and they all began chattering at once, their voices trailing away as they climbed the stairwell.

Alisabeth announced she needed to check on the blacksmith's wife, who had delivered a son the night before.

"Do ye mind if I follow along? Douglas has been praising yer ministrations since dawn." Calum whistled to his dogs and they padded behind. "Gideon, would ye like to hold a newborn bairn? There's nothing quite like it to make a man feel humble."

Though he had no experience with babies, in fact hadn't given them much thought until his sisters were married, the encouraging look in Lissie's eyes decided for him. "Why not? It will give me good practice for Etta's baby. I'll have my own one day, I suppose."

They left the castle, proceeded through the garden, and turned in the opposite direction of the stables. Several stone houses with thatched roofs stood in a row, each with a small garden plot behind. "I provide housing for the families who work for me. This is Douglas's fifth bairn but his first son. He's been crowing like a rooster."

Lissie knocked at the door then opened it a crack. "May we come in? The MacNaughton has come with his blessings." There was a shuffling of feet and then a huge burly man with wild red curls and a short-cropped beard filled the door frame.

"Calum! Welcome, welcome." Douglas slapped the chieftain on the back and pulled him to a long table in the center of the room.

Gideon realized with a start that he'd never been in a cottage of the lower class. Yet his grandfather made himself comfortable at the table as if he was a familiar visitor. As if there were no class differences between them. The floor was packed dirt and there was only one main space on the ground floor. Several windows let in weak light. At the far end of the room was a small bed—by Gideon's standard—with a dark-haired woman in her twenties and a baby with bright red fuzz sprouting from its head. Opposite them was a fireplace with an iron kettle hanging above a small fire.

As he adjusted to the dim interior, he saw the walls were made of dry stone. He'd heard of this, and seen some from a distance after crossing the border, but had not inspected any close up. The stones were stacked without any mortar to bind them, and shelves were somehow attached between the layers. A ladder stood at the opposite end of the bed, leading to a loft where he assumed the offspring must sleep. Due to the upstairs, only half of the home enjoyed the full height of the ceiling.

Douglas pulled three glasses from the wooden shelf that also held silver Sheffield plates. There were no bowls but the plates were deep enough to hold a stew or porridge. He retrieved a bottle and poured a dram of whiskey for each of them, a proud grin on his face.

"To bairns and sons and wives that never stop lovin' ye," roared the blacksmith. Both Scots tipped back their heads and drank down the liquor in one swallow. Gideon followed, wondering how many toasts he would be obligated to drink. He didn't relish a long ride if he was half foxed.

Calum set the glass on the table. "Lissie, are ye finished? May I give the blessing?"

"Aye, all is well." Lissie kissed the woman on the cheek then took the baby and handed him to the MacNaughton.

"The bairn looks even tinier in those huge paws." Lissie smiled. Her brandy-colored eyes were warm with affection as she gazed on the large Scot and the tiny babe.

Holding the bairn in front of him, rocking it slightly, Calum began an old Gaelic blessing. "Gum bi a' bheatha a' frasadh ort, a naoinein bhig; an fhallaineachd, an ionracas is an sonas mar thiodhlacan." He leaned down and kissed the child on the forehead.

"What did he say?" Gideon asked in a whisper.

"May your life be fruitful, little bairn. Health, honesty, and happiness be yer gifts." Tears shown in her eyes as she interpreted.

"Does he do this for every boy?"

"Aye," she answered, "for all the bairns. Each one is a blessing, no matter the sex."

Something stirred in Gideon's chest as he watched her expression. Happy yet sad. Yes, melancholy. But why, if she was carrying a child of her own? He wanted to pull her to him, hold her, and tell her all would be well. Instead, he clasped his hands behind his back and nodded. Had he ever been privy to such a touching scene? His father had painted the Scots as stern, superstitious, and uneducated. His mother's family an exception to the rule. It pained Gideon that his father might have been wrong, but the images he'd carried in his mind and those he'd seen since his arrival did not match up.

When they left the house, Alisabeth ran back to the castle. "I'll meet ye at the stables," she called to them over her shoulder and disappeared.

The men were soon followed by Gavin and the deer-hounds at their heels. "Can I ride Black Angus? Granny says he's big enough to put a saddle on."

The head groom, leading out a pair of chestnut horses to hook up to the carriage, scowled at his child. "Dinna be pestering the MacNaughton, son. He could squash ye with one boot if ye get under foot, and I wouldna blame him," his father warned. "And stop sneakin' oatcakes to the dogs, or I'll tell Granny not to let ye in the kitchens. I see yer pocket full of crumbs."

The boy ducked his head in apology, pulled the remaining pieces of griddle cake from his britches, and popped them in his mouth. Then he grabbed a brush and began helping his father curry the horses.

Gideon followed Calum into the stone barn. Since they were alone, it was a good time to bring up the subject on his mind since London. "Can I ask you about my mother's dreams?"

His grandfather paused then asked quietly, "The visions?"

Gideon nodded.

"She's always had them, though we keep it to ourselves. People are still afraid of witches, ye ken. It's one of three abilities passed down for centuries through our ancestors, the Dalais clan." He turned and looked Gideon straight in the eye. "And ye have the gift of Truth."

"Why do you say that? Because I'm a good judge of men? I have an inherent talent to know if they are lying?" He snorted. "Then I believe there are more witches out there than we realize."

"Don't make light of it, lad. Ye'll realize what's in yer soul when the time comes. And ye willna be laughing then." He slapped Gideon on the back. "It's yer ma's responsibility to pass on the story to the next generation, to tell ye the Dalais legend. Ye might find it quite interesting."

"It shall make a good nighttime adventure, I'm sure."

The old man threw a rope over the neck of a glossy bay

and led him out of the stall. He tossed another rope to Gideon, who caught it. "Do ye saddle your own mount?"

Calum stopped, surprise registering on his face. "Of course. Anything goes wrong on a ride, a man should only have himself to blame. Would ye trust another to yer own safety?"

"I haven't thought about it, to be honest, but you have a good point. Our grooms have always taken care of it."

"Ye do ken how to put on a saddle?" Disgust clouded his grandfather's eyes. "Tell me Charles showed ye at one point."

"The only physical tasks my father instructed me in was hunting, fishing, and shooting. Everything else came from a tutor." He shrugged. "However, I practically lived in the stables as a boy and was always under foot. Much like young Gavin there. I'm more than capable of taking care of myself."

Relief showed on Calum's face before an ornery smile curved his mouth. "Weel, that's fortunate. In that case, ye can get Lissie's mare readied also. And no sidesaddle—she's a Highland lass to the hilt and willna ride lopsided."

That stopped him cold. Such a fetching girl rode astride? Did she wear breeches or just hike up her dress? He grinned. Scotland was growing on him.

***

Alisabeth picked up her deep blue skirts and ran through the garden, delighted that Maeve had invited her to join them. The nightmares still haunted her, and each day she wore herself out, hoping to fall into a dreamless sleep. A ride on her favorite mare, instead of a bumpy conveyance, would be just the thing. A day next to the handsome-as-sin Lord Stanfeld was icing on the cake. It wasn't right, her conscience poked at her, but the man did take her mind off her troubles. It was harmless enough to enjoy a peek here or there. A younger image of Calum, she now understood why Peigi's eyes still sparkled when she looked at her husband. If Peigi was remembering him as a young man…

She slowed to a walk just before coming in sight of the barn. *Show Lord Stanfeld that Scottish ladies are as refined and graceful as the English,* she thought. *Well, certainly as graceful.*

Her mare, Faerie, stood patiently, her white coat and yellow mane glistening in the sun. Calum must have seen to the horse for her, as the men stood ready to mount. Lord Stanfeld wore those snug breeches that molded to his muscular legs. His sienna brown riding jacket emphasized the broad shoulders. She placed a hand on her stomach as something inside jumped. Why did he have such an effect on her? This queasy excitement was a new feeling, and one she'd never had with Ian.

"Just in time, lass," called Calum, mounting his bay gelding. "The carriage should be around with the girls any time now."

Lord Stanfeld held Faerie's reins. "Would you like assistance up, my lady?"

She bit her lip to hold off the laughter at "my lady." What would he say if he saw her grab the mane and leap onto a horse bareback? Faint dead away, most likely. *Refinement. Remember refinement.* "Why yes, I thank ye."

He cupped his hand and bent slightly. The muscles strained against his jacket as he waited. Her stomach fluttered again. Under her skirt, she wiped the bottom of her soft leather shoe against her stocking then placed it in his palm. It wouldn't due to get his expensive gloves dirty. With a gentle push, Alisabeth settled into the saddle and straightened her skirt.

She watched as he reached for his reins and mane, placed a boot in his stirrup, and mounted his huge black gelding in one fluid motion. The beast was twice the size of her mare, alert but calm. Lord Stanfeld was at ease in the saddle, and his confidence conveyed to the animal beneath. The horse snorted and pawed the dirt, but it quickly ceased with a slight tug on the bit and pressure to his girth. Lissie was impressed.

The carriage approached, a driver in the clan plaid clicking to the pair of chestnuts as they came around the drive. The vehicle was painted in the MacNaughton colors with the main body a dark green, blue trim, and their crest with the red circular keep painted on the door. Peigi opened the shutter and stuck her head out. "Last one there eats scraps!" The driver cracked his whip and the team lunged forward at a canter.

CHAPTER SIX

"On the road from the City of Skepticism, I had to pass through the Valley of Ambiguity."

— ADAM SMITH

*C*alum guffawed. "That woman of mine doesna give up. Never have I seen a more competitive female. Or one with such a fine appetite." He winked at Lissie. "Nothing worse than a female who picks at her food, pretending to be ladylike when she's starvin' like the forest critters after a long winter."

The threesome caught up with the vehicle and settled into an easy pace. Calum put his fingers to his mouth and let out a shrill whistle. The hounds came bounding behind them.

"Lord Stanfeld, are those scars on your horse's withers?" Alisabeth frowned. This could change her opinion of the earl. Yet the animal didn't seem abused.

"I'm afraid so, though they're fading. I bought him at an auction, the owner saying he was too addlebrained to be broke." He shook his head. "I've found that an animal with intelligence is often considered mulish. He responds well to a light hand and fair treatment. In fact, he's become one of my favorite mounts."

She nodded. "So you saved him from a worse fate. Ye are fond of animals, my lord?"

"I must admit I have an affinity with horses. I've been riding since the age of three, or so I'm told. As for other animals, we've always had packs of foxhounds for the hunt, but Father did not approve of them in the house." He shrugged. "And I insist you call me Gideon. It doesn't seem right when I've been granted permission to call you by your given name."

Lissie smiled when she saw him eyeing her boots in the stirrups. "Do all ladies in England ride sidesaddle, my-er, Gideon?"

"Many don't ride at all, but yes, those that do prefer the side saddle. Do you not find it exerting, being astride?"

"On the contrary, it's much easier to maintain balance when jumping. I canna imagine sailing across a stream with one leg cocked up in front of me."

Calum chuckled. "Ye should see the lass without a saddle. Now that's a sight."

Gideon looked at her with renewed interest. "Indeed? I would enjoy seeing you ride bareback." His lips twitched and she wondered what images ran through his mind. "The Highlands are more like another world than a place just across the border. Life isn't so…restrictive."

"Do ye like the change?" It was Alisabeth's turn to study him. "Or do ye long for the constraints that keep yer English world orderly and familiar?"

"Ha! There's my plain spoken lass." Calum gathered his

reins. "Let's see who gets to that crop of trees first. Ready?" He leaned over his horse's muscled neck. "Go!"

Alisabeth let out a squeal as she dug her heels into Faerie's sides. Gideon barely touched his gelding, and the horse took off like a fox chased by hounds. He easily won and all three were panting when they halted at the pines.

"Ye ride well, my lord," she admitted as she caught her breath. "Calum doesna like to lose."

Gideon shook his head. "I must say, I'm surprised, Grandfather. You're more fit than most of the gentlemen at Hyde Park. That was quite a lengthy gallop."

"And that's meant to be a compliment?" He reached over and slapped his grandson on the back. "Those dandies wouldna last a week here. I'd make sure of it."

The carriage rumbled up behind them, and the women got out to stretch their legs and take care of necessities. Calum whistled again and the dogs jumped off the back of the carriage. Gideon thought of the tigers, or rear coachmen, often employed in England.

"So Scottish tigers have fur and tails. I imagine they settle for scraps instead of a wage?"

"And much more dependable," added Glynis. "If we were set upon, those scraggly dogs would die for us. A paid hand may run to save his own skin. If only they'd get the knack of opening a door."

They spread out a blanket and opened the basket. Maeve passed a small mutton pie to Gideon, who turned it over and gave it a sniff. His mother giggled and nibbled at her own. He watched her and did the same, followed by a healthy bite. "This is delicious," he mumbled as he chewed. "Are there more?"

Peigi handed him another then pulled out a blade and cut hunks of cheese and bread. The deerhounds stayed at the edge of the picnic, snatching scraps tossed their way. Two skins of wine were passed around and Alisabeth lay back, closing her eyes. Ian would have enjoyed this day. And with that one thought, her heart hurt again. *No crying, ye silly ninny. It's a bonny day and he'd be cross if ye didna enjoy it,* she told herself.

As they packed up, Gideon offered to water the horses. Maeve waved a hand at both Lissie and her son. "Why dinna ye both take the horses down to the brook. There's a bonny view."

The water gurgled and splattered, rushing over mossy boulders, tadpoles shooting this way and that. The horses lowered their heads, slurping at the cold water. Alisabeth shielded her eyes then handed him her horse's lead rope. She stepped out onto a flat stone and pointed out the holly and hazel that grew on the fertile slopes to the east.

"The beauty of this land surprises me. I had expected the landscape to be rugged, but not this unique combination of lush green and jagged rock." He transferred both ropes to one hand and held the other out as she turned to jump back onto the grass. "Let me help you. It looks slick—"

At that moment, her boot slipped from under her. He grabbed her arm with strong fingers and pulled her toward him, her body slamming into his. Lissie's fingers grasped at his tailcoat as she struggled to regain her balance. The butterflies in her stomach flittered dangerously as the lean, hard muscles of his thighs pressed against her. The top of her head reached just under his chin. His chest rose and fell, his breath stirring her hair. She lifted her head just as he was looking down. Their faces were so close, she could have kissed his chin.

The crystal blue eyes darkened and his gaze lowered. Lissie's breath caught in her throat, her body frozen. *Saints and sinners, he's going to kiss me.* One of the horses pulled on its lead to reach a clump of grass. Gideon turned his head for a brief moment. Just enough time to step back and put distance between them. "Thank ye for saving me from a fall. It's a warm day, but I wouldna have liked being sodden the rest of the ride."

He bowed, a playful grin on his face, but his eyes were serious and dark with an emotion she didn't understand yet shared. With a hand to her stomach, Alisabeth picked up the stray rope and led the horse back to the clearing.

The sun cast its warm rays upon the party and the rest of the trip passed quickly. From the carriage, Peigi told Gideon her favorite Scottish lore. Calum explained how the landscape had changed from crofting to livestock during the Highland Clearances. The crofters had forfeited their land to the rich, who had combined the small parcels into large grazing pastures. Sheep now dotted the rocky green hills instead of grain.

"This is why weaving is so vital to us. Our wool is sent to the factory in Glasgow, where it's cheaper to have it turned into cloth. We still have some that work in their home, to provide us with our tartans and plaids, but the majority is done in the weaving shed with 18 water looms." The old man looked up at the sky. "I had chosen a different site for the mill but yer father insisted on Glasgow with the influx of Irish immigrants, many of them weavers. Water was another of his mandates so we built along the Clyde. He said power looms would replace handlooms some day. The earl had a sense for business, I'll give him that."

Lady Stanfeld told several stories of when she was a girl, and Lissie realized Gideon was hearing them for the first time. It struck her odd that his mother would not have shared childhood memories with her son.

"Didna yer mother tell ye stories when ye were a boy?" she asked.

"No, my father didn't like her to talk about her childhood.

I know it sounds harsh, but he didn't want our heads filled with fantasy and legends." He sighed. "I'm learning his decisions weren't always in our best interest."

"She must have truly loved him to give so up so much. I dinna ken if I could do that."

He was thoughtful before he answered. "Yes, she loved him deeply—stayed in full mourning for a year. Said it was to respect his English rules, but I think it took that long for her to grieve."

"I can understand that."

Gideon reached over and laid his hand over hers. "My apologies. That was thoughtless of me."

"We all are grieving so I am in good company."

"I'm sure the babe is a comfort."

Confused, she pulled up the reins. "What babe?"

"I thought you"—his face grew red—"were with child?"

A second stab to her heart. She shook her head, unable to form the words.

He rubbed a palm over his face. "Forgive me, I did not mean to cause you more pain. I assumed that was why you had stayed with my grandparents."

"Don't blame yerself. I'm just a wee sensitive. It was a disappointment not only for me but the clan. And I stayed because... Glynis wasna ready to be alone, and I hadna decided what to do." She wiped at the tear that slipped out the corner of one eye.

"That explains the look on your face this morning when Grandfather held the baby."

His intuitiveness surprised her. He had more of the MacNaughton blood in him than he thought. "Being with Ian is the only future I've ever known. It was snatched from me so suddenly, I'm still..."

"Struggling to find your place?" He nodded in understanding. "Why not go home?"

"My family would welcome me, to be sure. Yet it seems as if I'd be walking backwards into the past rather than forward into the future." She shrugged. "Sounds foolish, I know."

He shook his head. "Not at all. Your world spun upside down in an instant. While I feel an emptiness from his loss, it doesn't change my life. But you are a strong woman. You'll find the answers."

They continued in companionable silence, while she pondered this unexpected empathy in Gideon Stanfeld. By early afternoon, they reached Dunderave. More dry stone houses and thatched roofs lined the main street. At one end of the village was a blacksmith and small dry goods and specialty store, at the other was a *kirk*, or church. A crowd had gathered and the minister, Reverend Robertson, stepped forward to greet them. "It is good to see ye, Calum. We heard Maeve found her way home again."

The person in question flung open the carriage door. An older woman with streaks of white in her orange hair pushed through the throng. "My sweet Maeve, let me look at ye."

"Oh, Moira, ye havena changed a bit," cried the countess as she threw her arms around the tiny woman in a fierce hug. "Where are yer children and grandchildren?"

"All here. Ye'll come to the house and sit a spell?"

The voices rose as Lady Stanfeld recognized each villager and was introduced to family members. Calum bellowed at a lad to take the horses, flapped an arm at the ruckus, and pulled Gideon and the minister away from the group. The villagers had been to MacNaughton Castle for the funeral, so the MacNaughton did not need to stay for the gossip. Lissie watched the men disappear into the minister's house, knowing whiskey would be part of their conversation.

"Lissie, come with us," called the countess. "Help me remember all the new names."

"Yes, my lady." Alisabeth picked up her skirts and moved to her side.

"Please, call me Maeve. Do I still look like Lady Stanfeld?"

She took in the local material and familiar plaid adorning Maeve's shoulders. "No, my lady, ye dinna." Taking her elbow, she led the older woman toward the row of houses. "Where shall we begin?"

***

Gideon took his second "wee" dram of scotch whiskey and held back the shudder. Robust spirits for a stout people. He looked around the modest home and thought of the elegant home of the bishop near his English estate. A small hearth graced the far wall, peat glowing in the grate. The walls were layers of stone, and flagstone had been dug into the packed dirt floor. Material wealth did not seem a priority in this strange land.

They sat at a small wooden table, scarred and stained from years of use, with two back chairs and a stool. The minister had insisted his guest take the chairs while he cheerfully perched his thin frame on the three-legged stool. The hounds lounged near the door. Gideon again found himself socializing in peculiar surroundings. Squalor, his father would have called these conditions. Yet here in the Highlands, these men were his equal.

The minister had taken the stool to be hospitable toward his new guest. He offered the chair to his grandfather in deference to his position and reputation, which the chieftain had earned. Gideon realized he wanted *that* type of esteem, not the kind one was born to and given without thought. His privileged life had created a selfish man with a high opinion of himself. It jarred him. He *was* his father, pompous and proud. But he wanted to be like his grandfather.

"There's a bit of an issue that will need yer attention before ye go, Calum." Reverend Robertson poured more of the fiery liquid into Calum's glass. "It seems a few of Rory MacDunn's sheep got mixed in with another flock, or didna, according to Ross Craigg. He says MacDunn stole them. As ye ken, MacDunn's elder son was flogged several years ago for stealing a prize rooster, and Craigg has since blamed the clan for mishaps not of their doing. To keep the peace, I took the sheep until ye arrived. They will abide by whatever ye say."

"They are both family. MacDunns are part of the MacNaugton clan and the Craiggs are Lissie's family." Calum nodded at Gideon. "Not much different than yer responsibilities as an earl. It's the hardest part of my position, deciding who lies or exaggerates. The lines of truth are not always clear."

"I disagree. It can always be found in a man's eyes if you look deep enough."

The minister arched an eyebrow. "An English philosopher, eh? Ye may come in verra handy for these proceedings."

Gideon opened his mouth to decline but a pounding from outside had the minister trotting for the door. Two men walked in, pulled their caps, and tried to smooth their tousled hair. With a bow of their heads, they greeted Calum.

"I hear there's a difference of opinion," began Calum. "Why do yer sheep not have a keel or lug mark?"

The minister whispered to Gideon, "We use common pasture. Keeling is a paint that tells us from a distance who the beasties belong to. Or marks are cut into their ears. Each farmer has his own particular notch."

Since he had recently invested in sheep, Gideon found this all fascinating. As the men explained how these three sheep might have escaped the keeling, it seemed the sheep did have lug marks. As they made their way around the back, Calum ordered the dogs to stay a respectable distance from the group. The men examined the animals loaded in a wagon.

The Craiggs used a single V notch, and the MacDunns used two Vs. All the sheep had the MacDunn marking.

Calum frowned. "It's no mystery to me. They all have the MacDunn lug marks."

"The second mark has been added," said Ross Craigg accusingly. "Look closer, ye'll see one of the Vs is more recent."

Calum rubbed one ewe's ear, his eyes narrow. "MacDunn, what kind of thievery is this? Do ye think my brain's no bigger than this sheep?"

"I swear to ye by all that's holy, I didna add that mark." MacDunn bellowed, panic in his voice.

It was one thing to argue over livestock that had been mixed together. It was another to steal. If the marks had been added, it was proof of deceit. In England, men were hanged for such an offense. The best-case scenario was another flogging. Either way, the atmosphere had gone from bright to dark.

Gideon stared at the man. "You're saying you never tampered with those ewes, and no one under your employ touched them to add a mark?"

The man shook his head adamantly. He was telling the truth, it showed in his countenance. He'd gamble that MacDunn had not been in on this plot.

"Liar! Ye did and ye'll hang for it," cried Craigg. His dark coloring and light brown eyes resembled Alisabeth, but the similarity ended there. He had a bulbous nose with blue veins running through it—a sign of a heavy drinker. The deep lines across his forehead and around his eyes gave the appearance of a permanent scowl. This man had a malicious countenance, and Gideon did not trust him.

Calum towered over the men, his presence demanding and his voice deadly quiet. "I will make the judgments here.

We are in Scotland not England. I'll not hang a man for a bit of wool. But I'll flog him myself if he's guilty of lying."

Craigg glared at Calum, and as the irate man balled his hands into fists, Gideon saw it. The hatred and the deceit in his eyes. Without a doubt, he knew the man had added a mark to his own sheep. But why?

"The MacDunns have a reputation for pilfering. Ye would take his word over mine? My cousin Alisabeth lives under yer roof, and ye side with this common criminal?" Craigg sneered. "Or are ye getting weak in yer old age and afraid the MacDunns will retaliate?"

"I take offense on both counts, Ross. Our clans have been at peace for too long for ye to speak such filth."

Calum's neck went red. Gideon could see the tick in his jaw. This confrontation was turning dangerous. His father had told Gideon of the constant blood feuds and raiding between the clans. But he suddenly knew there was more to this than the theft of sheep. He looked into Craigg's eyes and held his gaze. The other man grew more uncomfortable the longer Gideon stared. And then he knew. The Truth slapped him in the face and shook him to the core. There was a girl and boy involved, a young couple. They had fled from their parents. He ran a shaky hand through his hair. This was not information one could guess or assume without knowing the people involved. Good God, he did have an ability. How would he explain it?

He cleared his throat. "Grandfather, could I speak to you and Reverend Robertson for a moment? I might be able to help but would like to confer in private."

The minister nodded, relief in his eyes. "Craigg, stay here with the ewes while we go inside. MacDunn, ye can wait out front."

Calum beckoned Black Angus, pointed to Ross Craigg

and ordered, "Fuirich!" The dog moved next to the other man, standing sentry.

They walked around the cottage once again. Behind them, Craigg bellowed, "What kind of trickery is this?" Angus growled low, stopping any further complaints.

Before entering the house, Calum left Brownie with the other man. Reverend Robertson wiped his forehead with his sleeve. "This is not what I expected, Calum. I apologize when ye've come to issue invitations and bring Maeve here for a visit."

"Och, it's no one's fault. And it's my duty as chieftain. So, let's see what my grandson has to say."

Gideon wasted no time. "The man named Craigg is lying. He added those marks to incriminate MacDunn."

Calum rubbed his jaw. "Ye are sure?"

Reverend Robertson seemed leery. "We're to convict a man because ye have a feeling about one of them? I canna say this is a good idea, Calum."

He wiped his sweaty palms against his breeches. "No, it's more than that. It's"—an imperceptible move of his grandfather's head told him others did not know—"a skill I possess. I can read a man and tell if he's cutting a sham." He turned back to Calum. "He wants revenge because… I'd *wager* it has to do with his daughter and MacDunn's son."

"The thief? I can understand Craigg's ire," admitted Calum.

The minister stroked his chin. "No, MacDunn's youngest boy was courting the Craigg girl. He claimed they were handfasted. When Craigg found out, he beat her until she denied giving her consent then forbade her to see the lad again. They tried to elope but MacDunn caught them, sent the girl back, and locked his boy in the cellar for a week. But that was last spring."

Gideon's pulse thudded in his neck. He'd been right. How the hell had he managed it?

"Early spring or late spring?" asked his grandfather.

"May Day when they eloped. Why?"

Calum's face split into a wide grin. He slapped Gideon on the back. "God's teeth, lad. Ye're brilliant."

He went to the door. "MacDunn, get that boy of yers over here. The one who's sweet on the Craigg girl. He marched to the back. "Ross, ye bring yer daughter here within the hour. If ye dinna, I'll come and find ye and flog ye myself."

An hour later, father and son and father and daughter stood in the minister's house. The fathers looked murderous. The children looked nervous.

Calum looked at the tall, lean lad. "Hamish, how old are ye?"

"Seventeen, sir."

"Do ye love the lass?"

Hamish gave the pretty dark-haired girl a sideways glance and nodded. "With my last breath."

"Weel, let's hope it doesna come to that. Nessie, do ye love him?"

She sniffed, picked up the edge of a voluminous apron, and wiped at the tears trickling down her cheeks. "With all my heart and soul."

A growl came from her father, and he knocked her on the side of her head. She stumbled and Hamish lunged for the older man. Both deerhounds jumped to their feet with a snarl, teeth bared and hackles up. MacDunn wrapped his son in a bear hug, the boy kicking and throwing punches in the air.

"Touch the lass again, Craigg, and ye'll have my fist in yer face. Ye understand?"

He grunted in reply, still scowling at Nessie.

Calum smiled at the girl. "Lass, are ye with child?"

One hand rubbed the side of her head where her father had smacked her. Now the other hand went instinctively to her belly, showing a swell under the ample material as she nodded her head.

"Ye no good whore!" cried her father. She shoved a fist in her mouth to stifle a sob.

"Weel, this isna so complicated after all, is it?" Calum crossed his arms over his chest and grinned. "Ross, it seems ye have two choices. Ye give yer daughter consent to marry the lad so the bairn has a father, and I don't flog ye. Or I flog ye, and tell the whole village what's conspired here."

"Ye will not tell me what to—"

"Make yer choice."

With gritted teeth, he spit out, "Marry the little brògan. She's dead to me."

"Fine," said Calum in a cheery voice. "And as dowry, she'll bring along anything her ma would have given her. As a wedding gift, ye'll give them the sheep in the back, seeing they already have MacDunn's lug mark. Agreed?"

"Aye," Ross growled.

"Rory MacDunn, will ye take the lass in? They canna live with the Craiggs."

"Aye," Rory said, giving a sharp elbow to his son. "See what comes from trusting the chieftain? Justice."

"And a lovely wife," added the minister, also ignoring the irate father.

"And there'll be no laying of hands on the lass before she leaves yer home. Do we have an understanding?"

Craigg jerked his head in assent but looked directly at Gideon, his eyes blazing with hate. "I dinna ken why this is any of yer affair or how ye were privy to my business. But it's not over yet."

"Mind yerself, Ross. Ye're lucky the MacNaughton is a

generous man," the minister said grimly. "Dinna put more strife upon yerself or yer family. Let it go."

Calum smiled at the young couple. "We came with an invitation to MacNaughton Castle, a cèilidh to celebrate the return of my daughter, Maeve. I'm thinking we may as well as have a wedding while we're at it."

CHAPTER SEVEN

"Lord, help my poor soul."

— EDGAR ALLEN POE

Early October
MacNaughton Castle

eigi had not taken kindly to a wedding added on to her agenda. She capitulated once Calum explained the circumstances. Ross was known for his cruel streak, making him a black sheep in the Craigg clan. His daughter Nessie would be better off with the MacDunns. That made Alisabeth giggle. A black sheep, and it was sheep that caught him up. The mirth faded as she remembered the rumors of his simmering anger and mutters of betrayal.

Gideon had relayed the details on the trip home, and she still wondered how the men had managed to uncover the mystery in so short a time. Oh, how she would have enjoyed seeing the look on her cousin's face when Calum threatened to flog him. That was why he was chieftain. Few men could make threats like the MacNaughton. Fewer men could carry them out, and he was known for keeping his word—good or bad.

Alisabeth pulled her stockings up, tied the garters, and slid on her leather shoes. Smoothing down her satin skirts of deep blue, the color reminded her of a clear midnight sky. The sheer matching lace covered her hair, pulled high on her head and falling in ringlets. She arranged the plaid about her shoulders and tugged at the curls about her face. With a sigh, she approved her image in the looking glass and twisted the band still on her finger. The circle of continuous love. She said a silent prayer that tears would not mar the day when the young couple exchanged their rings.

The last three weeks of preparation had been hectic, and now it was time to celebrate. Last Sunday Reverend Robertson had announced the union of Nessie and Hamish for the third time. Today they would be married at the small chapel on the MacNaughton land. The meat was prepared and refreshments ready. Venison and pig sizzled on spits. Dishes for the rest of the courses, along with baked goods, were cooling or simmering in the kitchen. Alisabeth had made the bridescake herself since her cousin had refused to let Nessie's mother attend the ceremony. Her own parents would be standing in their place for the Craigg clan.

In the main hall, Peigi gave last minute orders to house-maids and cooks. "Be certain there is plenty of wine and ale. My husband willna be happy if we run out of either. Once the food is served, ye may join in the festivities. Keep at least two on duty throughout the day and evening to check the pitchers and platters." Guests already filled the hall for the late morning ceremony. She spotted Alisabeth across the room and beckoned with a wave.

"It looks splendid, Peigi. Nessie willna believe such finery is for her wedding day." Tressle tables lined one wall with small pies, breads, and fruit compotes. More tressles were set up with benches for eating and visiting, white linen spread across the wooden boards with candles and crystal water bowls for washing. Maeve and Glynis had seen to the table decorations and had personally supervised the making of the entwined circles of marzipan. The sugar creation sparkled and shed twinkling crumbs along the length of the linen. On the dais, silver goblets and plates had been set out for the guests of honor and their hosts.

"It is a celebration for my daughter as well. Her visit is passing much too quickly, but I take comfort in the fact she'll return again." A whistle from the courtyard silenced the hall.

"The bride is here. Everyone outside for the procession to the kirk," called Maeve, her cheeks flushed. "Gideon, give me yer arm!"

He stood at the entrance of the hall, his wine-colored tail-coat fitting snugly across his shoulders with an embroidered gold waistcoat and matching trousers. His intense gaze searched the room. Alisabeth's breath caught when he found her. His blue eyes sparkled like a loch in springtime then his smile turned her stomach to jelly. He made his way through the room, offered his mother an arm then the other to Lissie. She took it with a grateful smile, her fingers light upon the hard muscle beneath the cloth, and joined the guests in the courtyard.

Waiting in the wagon, Nessie glowed in her muslin rose gown. Her shining dark hair fell loose over her shoulders, crowned with a ringlet of pink flowers.

"Right foot forward for good luck," someone yelled.

"Yer father hated these old wives' tales. I've almost forgotten some of them," laughed Maeve to Gideon as the girl stepped down with the correct foot.

A piper led the procession, followed by neighbors sprinkling a trail of flower petals, and then the groom. The bagpipes serenaded the party as they stopped in front of the kirk. Hamish's best man, Ian's brother Lachlan, escorted Nessie. He had the same chestnut hair as his mother Glynis but his grandfather's sapphire blue eyes. Lachlan had arrived from Glasgow the day before. It had been a disappointment that Lachlan's younger brother and sister had been unable to attend, but many other clan members had made the journey. The men were splendid in their tartans with dress sporrans and glinting dirks, hair clean and shining, beards trimmed or faces shaved. The women wore their best satin or silk dresses or earasaids, plaids over their shoulders or across their chest, depending on their station.

At the ancient kirk door, Reverend Robertson welcomed the couple. Hamish gave Nessie a sheaf of wheat, and she gave him a piece of woven cloth.

Gideon whispered in Lissie's ear, "What's the meaning of that?"

"It represents their promise to each other to provide for their home."

Next the couple exchanged a dagger and a bible. "This shows his physical pledge and her spiritual pledge to defend their home."

The guests crowded into the small church. Near the altar, Lachlan's sword hissed as he unsheathed it to make a circle around the couple. As he did so, the couple said in unison,

"The Mighty Three, my protection be, encircle me,

You are around my life, my love, my home.

Encircle me, O sacred three, the Mighty Thee."

Reverend Robertson finished the ceremony and presented the couple to the crowd. "You may kiss the bride." Hamish took Nessie's hands in his and stared at her for a long moment. Then he dipped his head, brushed his lips lightly across her mouth, and leaned his forehead against hers. The intensity of the love between them shone brightly and brought tears to Alisabeth's eyes.

For the first time, she regretted what she and Ian had *not* shared. Yes, they had loved each other but not like this couple. That pureness had been missing; that passion exploding not only in physical desire but also emotional need. The devotion and tenderness for one another that was so obvious between Nessie and Hamish had not been part of her marriage. She and Ian had settled for deep affection and friendship.

Panic seized her as her fingers searched again for the silk gloves in her pocket. Ian could have found this kind of love with another if she had refused the betrothal. Had she denied him a chance of true happiness in his short life? Pain stabbed her chest. She was young and still had years in front of her. The thought that Fate may yet send her a love such as theirs sent a nauseating wave of guilt through her stomach.

I'm so verra sorry if I robbed ye of such an opportunity. Ye ken how much I cared for ye, she silently told him. Alisabeth fought back tears when a blurry handkerchief appeared in front of her. She blinked twice, sniffled, and gratefully took it.

"It's usually my mother that needs this at a wedding so I came prepared," whispered Gideon, squeezing her hand gently as she grasped the cloth in her palm. Her whole body tingled from his touch. The sensation replaced the pang of remorse in heart and put a smile on her face. She could not change the past so she would think only happy thoughts and enjoy the day.

***

Gideon took his place on the dais next to his mother. They sat to the right of Calum and Peigi, the bride and groom on the left. Directly below, his aunt and cousin were seated with Alisabeth, her parents, and the MacDunn men.

Calum stood, raised his glass, and made a toast to family and clan. Then he passed the two-handled *quaich* down the table. The couple filled the ancient vessel with whiskey and moved to the table below. Hamish gave it to his father, who took a drink then offered it to Alisabeth's father, who did the same. The couple then drank from the cup, and the hall resounded with loud cheers.

"That particular cup is a family relic but the Quaich is a tradition in weddings of different clans. The two handles are for the joining of the families." Maeve lowered her voice. "Since Nessie's parents are not here, Lissie's have taken their place in the joining ritual."

Gideon found the entire ceremony intriguing. There seemed to be a reason or symbol for everything. His practical mind shook its head at some of the traditions, but another part of him embraced them. Customs bound these people together, gave them a common ground that transcended class or title. It was a comforting thought—that one belonged no matter his birth.

The afternoon became a gluttonous affair. Wine, ale, and food flowed. Gideon had never tasted venison so tender or vegetables so well-seasoned. Every dish tempted him—until a platter was presented to his grandfather.

"What in the devil is that?" he asked his mother. It looked like a roundish, oversized sausage.

"Haggis. Oh, ye are in for a treat. Heart, liver, lung…"

His stomach clenched.

"Boiled in a sheep's stomach," she added wickedly.

Calum took a polished blade to the bag, and the skin split, ground offal, oats and grains spilling out in a steaming heap. Much to Gideon's surprise, the spicy aroma was pleasant. He took a polite bite or two and gave the rest to his mother.

Once the meal was over, the music began. How a person could dance after so much food was baffling. In England, they danced and then ate at a later hour. The guests gathered in two long lines, couples across from one another, and the fiddler and small pipes took up a lively beat. The couples took turns weaving their way up and down the line, skipping to meet in the middle then back. It was similar to an English country-dance so Gideon knew he'd be able to muddle through a set if his mother asked.

"My dear, I've been meaning to ask ye a favor."

He smiled, assuming she wanted a partner for the next set. "Anything within my power, Mama," he answered generously as he took a drink.

"I'd like to bring Lissie home with us."

He spit out the red wine. "W-what?" Picking up a cloth, he wiped his chin and dabbed at the spreading stains on the white linen.

"Oh my, are ye all right?" she asked, pressing her lips together as her mouth curved ever so slightly. "I was thinking how lonely I get, and Etta won't be staying long once we return. She'll want to be home to have the baby. Ye'll be busy, and with winter approaching, it would be nice to have some female company. I didna realize how much I've missed it since the girls have all gone."

"I understand. You just took me by surprise. Why Lissie?" he asked, wondering how to make the pulse stop pounding in his head. It had been difficult enough the past weeks being so near her, and the image of that exquisite creature in his home…

"I've noticed the two of ye get along quite well. Ye play chess or cards most nights, ye sing well together, and she and I have the liveliest conversations. I thought it might be a nice distraction for ye also when ye're home." She smiled brightly and patted his hand. "I have a feeling it would be good for all of us."

"Only a feeling or did ye dream it?" His eyes narrowed. "We still need to have a conversation about that."

"Ye are right. *She* is the reason for my vision. The purpose for coming here." Maeve sighed. "I dinna ken why, but she has a part to play in whatever the future holds."

Is that why he was drawn to her? Why she invaded his sleep and his heart lifted when she entered the room? Gideon threw back the rest of his wine. Maybe he should stop searching for logical explanations until he was back in England. "So, one mystery explained but another yet to be solved?"

The groom's father appeared and bowed low over Maeve's hand. "Lady Stanfeld, ye are a vision tonight."

Or having one, Gideon thought ruefully.

"Rory MacDunn, it's been too long," his mother purred.

What was going on here? Was she flirting with this man?

"That is not of my doing, ye ken." He winked at her, a dimple showing in his cheek. "It seems we have something in common now, my lady."

"Aye, we do. Both of us widows."

"May I have the pleasure of the next dance?" His broad smile, perhaps the result of too much whiskey, crinkled the corners of his green eyes. "I would die a happy man tonight if I was to hold ye close for even a moment."

She stood with a dazzling smile then said over her shoulder, "Gideon, I do believe Lissie is in need of a partner." Maeve offered her hand to the towering Scot and glided onto the dance floor.

Heat reddened Gideon's neck. What the devil was going on with his mother? And how could she know of his attraction to Lissie when he was just realizing it himself. Alisabeth's pink cheeks told him she had overheard. He took comfort in their shared embarrassment and approached the table. "Would you care to dance?"

She fumbled in her pocket, closed her lids for a brief moment, and looked up at him. It had not been embarrassment that stained her smooth complexion. The pain in her eyes hit him like a punch to the gut. He had the urge to pull her to him, stroke her hair, and make her troubles disappear. But the expression passed so quickly, he wondered if he'd misread it.

"I would love to, my lord."

Her silky tone washed over him. Placing her fingers in his outstretched hand, he stiffened at the jolt of her skin against his. The slow burn began in his belly again, his body tense and hot. Nothing seemed strong enough to put out the fire. Gideon had never had such an intense reaction to a female. It unnerved him. Setting his shoulders straight, he was determined to act like a gentleman and pretend nothing was amiss.

The fiddler gave a warning note and the couples lined up. The pipes joined in and the first couple cast off. Gideon frowned as his mother went around him and back to MacDunn. He'd almost forgotten how graceful and light she was on her feet. An appreciative gleam also shone in MacDunn's eyes.

When it was his turn, Gideon moved around his neighbor and met Lissie in the middle. Their fingers clasped, and he saw her intake of breath as they circled one another. It was the same each time their hands touched. She must also feel it. By the end of the dance, they were both breathing rapidly. He was glad for the excuse of physical exertion, though he was too fit for one dance to tire him. And the way she rode a horse, so was Lissie.

He thanked her and returned to the dais. His mother soon followed, her laughter tinkling like a spoon against china. It pleased him to see her in such high spirits again but irritated him that it was a man who had achieved it. "Did you enjoy the dance?"

"Oh yes, immensely. And it seemed ye did as well." Maeve nodded her head to acknowledge a couple passing by. "What do ye think of my idea?" she asked, continuing to smile and nod at guests.

Gideon realized putting miles between them would not erase Lissie from his memory. She was beautiful, intelligent, full of life, and could spin a tale as well as his mother. Everything his father had told him to avoid in a wife. If she came back to England, he'd know if the attraction was purely Lissie or if it had something to do with the allure of the Highlands. He would bide his time and see where it led. There was no hurry; he was a young man with no dire need for an heir right away. "I think if it makes you happy, it makes me happy."

"It's settled then."

"What about Grandfather? Will Aunt Glynis let her go?" He had a suspicion this had all been discussed previously.

"Yer cousin Brodie will remain in the Highlands to help his mother since Lachlan has take Ian's place at the mill. And Glynis still has Bridget, though she behaves more like a son than a daughter. Da believes Lissie will heal faster if she is away from MacNaughton Castle." She patted his hand. "As I said, I have a feeling about her. She was meant to be a member of our clan so I'd like to support her if I can."

"When will you ask her?" Perhaps he could also help remove the pain from those tawny eyes.

"We leave next week so it must be soon."

Less than an hour passed and MacDunn returned for another dance. Mama's delight was infectious, and he searched the crowd for Lissie. He found her with the children, dancing in a circle around Gavin, who hopped and tapped his feet in the center.

"May I interrupt to request this reel?" He bowed low and was pleased to see her smile. She curtsied in response.

As they made their way to the group of dancers, Gideon leaned near her ear. "I have a secret. I've never danced a Scottish reel. Are they much different?"

"When we begin changing partners, it can get a bit confusing. Just hold out yer arm, and someone will send ye in the correct direction. The round is complete when we meet up again."

"I am in your hands, my lady."

Her giggle sent a flush of pleasure through him. Better than brandy on a cold winter night.

CHAPTER EIGHT

"There is nothing in the whole frame of man which seems to me so unaccountable as that thing called conscience."

— ROBERT BURNS

---

*G*ideon prayed he did not make a fool of himself. The fast-paced reel began in a circle, all participants holding hands. They split off into four lines, connected at the center, and moved in a clockwise direction but not with hands held. No, the dancers put their arms around each other's waist and twirled. It felt so natural to pull her against him, have her cling to him as the steps quickened and the momentum pushed their bodies closer together. When they separated, he missed her curves pressing next to his until the clasping and whirling began all over again. This time when the dance ended, he was truly out of breath. Lissie's chest heaved as she gulped in air, the smile on her lips so sincere and inviting, he almost dipped his head for a kiss. With extreme self-control, he restrained himself to a hand at the small of her back.

"I need some fresh air," he heard his mother exclaim. "Gideon, why don't you bring Lissie out with us?"

"Aye, that's a grand idea," agreed Alisabeth.

"Rory, would ye get a drink to soothe my parched throat?" Maeve rested a hand in the crook of his elbow, and said over shoulder, "We'll meet ye both in the garden."

Gideon held out his arm and Lissie accepted. Twilight had descended and a breeze stirred the leaves of bushes and plants. "So walks without a chaperone are permissible? At home, this would be scandalous."

"It's fine unless ye have some devious plot to kidnap or have yer way with me. But with yer mother coming soon, I dinna think ye'd risk it." She peered up at him, straight-faced but mischief sparkling in her amber eyes. "I didna think ye the type but still waters run deep as they say. We're told as children every Englishmen has at least a wee bit of villain in him."

He stopped and faced her. "Lissie! I can assure you—"

Her laughter hung on the night air. "The English have no sense of humor, I swear it."

"I'm offended. Of course we do. *I* do. It's just a more subtle humor. And I'll have you know, I pulled plenty of pranks at university."

Gideon heard a rustling sound at the edge of the garden. He paused at a stone bench. Guiding Lissie onto it, he peered into a dense grove of trees. "I believe there are faeries watching us from the branches."

She turned her head quickly, eyes squinted in concentration. "Where—" She smacked his arm as he sat down next to her chuckling. "Ye've proved yer point."

"I'm curious. Are Scottish women generally as educated

as you? The books you've read, the politics. It doesn't seem to fit with this life."

"We canna be learned without being pompous like the English?"

"Pompous?" He puffed out his chest and realized too late how it looked. With a guffaw, he admitted, "I suppose many of us give that impression."

"We are firm believers in education for both sexes. First, it was religious in nature. All of God's creatures should be able to read the bible." She shrugged. "My da doesna believe women's minds are inferior to men's, so I've been educated like a son except for going to university."

"I agree with your father." They sat for a moment, enjoying the quiet of the evening and the faint sounds of pipes and violin floating on the still air. She looked forward, a wistful expression in her golden eyes. Gideon leaned closer, breathing in the lavender scent of her skin and hair.

"Do you believe in romantic love?" she asked, her voice barely above a whisper. "The poets do. Yer mother does…"

Yes, he wanted to murmur in her ear. *You make me believe in things I never thought possible.* Instead he quoted Lord Byron:

"And on that cheek, and o'er that brow,
So soft, so calm, yet eloquent,
The smiles that win, the tints that glow,
But tells of days in goodness spent."

Alisabeth turned her face to him, her eyes searching his, their faces close.

. . .

"A mind at peace with all below,
    A heart whose love is innocent!"

Gideon tilted his head, focused on those full pink lips, knowing he could not deny himself a kiss. Just a kiss. He bent close, their breaths mingling—

A soft whimper jerked them from the moment. Alisabeth leapt to her feet. A rustle of leaves and another high-pitched moan, like an injured child or small animal. She picked up her skirts and moved around the bench.

"Lissie, wait. You don't know what it could be." Gideon mumbled a curse, both at the interruption and her disregard for safety as she hurried into the shadows.

"Gideon!" He looked down the dark garden path they had taken, barely illuminated by the castle lights, and saw a dark form moving toward him. A scream pulled his attention back to the small copse of trees. Without hesitation, he darted into the woods.

"Lissie!" The muted colors of her clothes made it hard to track her. Panic squeezed the breath from his lungs. "Lissie!"

From the corner of his eye, he saw the glint of a blade and knew the first true moment of terror in his life.

***

Alisabeth thought a child had wandered off from the cèilidh. Her heart went out to the poor thing. She was also thankful for the respite. Without a doubt, she would have kissed him. *Saints and sinners, ye're a wanton, disloyal—*

An arm went about her waist and pulled her off her feet. She let out a scream before a hand clamped over her mouth. Her feet kicked at the legs behind her, fingers scratching at the arms that held her so tight she could barely suck in a breath. A second dark figure loomed in front of her.

"Shut up and I'll let ye live, ye MacNaughton whore."

She froze. His face was hidden by the night, but she knew Ross Craigg's voice.

"Ye no-good, conniving piece of cow dung. Tell yer lick-spittle to put me down. Calum will have yer head for this."

The back of his hand sent her head spinning. She saw bits of light, and Ross' face came in and out of focus. An ache began in her jaw and threaded down her neck.

"Not before I have his grandson's."

Her body went still. "Ye've gone mad as a March hare."

"Lissie... Lissie!"

"Here comes the gentleman in question. Now remember ye're a Craigg for just a moment, and no harm will come to ye."

"Why?" She spit blood from her mouth. "Ye know ye'll never get away with murdering a MacNaughton, let alone an Englishmen. Ye'll have the law of Scotland *and* England after ye and me as a witness."

"Ye'd stand up for that fousome English pig over yer own kin? Then ye are no blood of mine."

"If you harm a hair on her head, I'll kill you. Slowly. Very slowly." The voice was deep, quiet, and deadly. "You know, we English have had centuries of practice."

Rage shone in Ross' eyes as he turned to confront the earl, only to be met with a fist to his face. Sprawled on the ground, he rubbed his jaw. "I'm not paying ye to keep my company. If he knocks me down again, slice the lass' throat," he said to the ruffian holding Alisabeth.

The man grunted in confirmation, his foul breath making her gag. He pulled her hands behind her back. She winced at the pain that radiated up her arms.

Ross Craigg rose, pulled a pistol from his belt, and pointed it at Gideon.

"I understand you hold no love for the MacNaughtons. But think of the consequences to the rest of your family."

Gideon held up his hands as if in surrender but took a step sideways, out of the direct path of the gun.

Hissss. Lachlan called from behind Ross, his sword drawn. "Stand down, Craigg. This canna end well for ye."

"Och, luck is on my shoulder. The grandiose Lachlan returned to take his brother's place. We'll take both of ye down."

Gideon again spoke softly, taking another sidestep toward Alisabeth. "You still haven't answered the lady's question. Why?"

"Her da"—he jerked his head at Alisabeth—"can taint his offspring with the MacNaughton's but I'll not be his toady. I never asked for peace between our clans. I should be head of the Craiggs."

"No one would ever follow such a cur," Alisabeth hissed.

"It doesna matter. Nessie's *my* property, not the chieftain's. I decide who my blood mixes with and who marries my daughter."

"So ye'll take the noose rather than see yer daughter married to a MacDunn? Ye've lost yer mind, mon." Lachlan moved his sword slowly back and forth as he crouched in preparation for the fight to come.

"I'll not take orders from the MacNaughton, who listens to a spawn of the devil." Ross sneered at Gideon. "Ye've been here a month, come into my village, and know my business. There's something unnatural about ye, and I intend to rid us all of that peculiar power. It's done enough harm, in my opinion." Ross spit on the ground in front of Gideon.

As he bent his head in disgust, Lachlan lunged forward. The sword sliced Craigg's hand, and the pistol tumbled to the ground. Ross drew his own sword and faced Lachlan. At the same time, Alisabeth kicked backward, knocking her captor off balance. As she hoped, it was enough time for Gideon. He seized the opening and landed a punch to the man's head.

She broke free. Her pounding heart sent waves of pain through her skull.

"Run, Lissie." The earl threw another punch before the other man's knuckles connected with his jaw, and they landed together in a heap on the hard earth. The rogue straddled Gideon and pushed his face into the dirt. Gideon's fingers crawled up his assailant's shirt, found his neck, and squeezed. The man raised an arm, a dagger clenched in his fist.

Terror gripped Alisabeth. Her heart constricted at the thought of another man she cared for dying before his time. Across the clearing, Lachlan and Ross stood nose to nose, swords crossed. Ross' shirt was torn and blood splashed down his kilt. Lachlan kicked him in the stomach and raised his blade. Ross charged, screaming like a mad boar.

Lissie dove for the pistol. Her body sprawled on the ground, dirt filling her mouth and stinging her eyes. The pungent smell of pine filled her nose as she rolled over on her back. She cringed at the sound of crunching bone as Gideon landed another punch to his attacker's jaw. Moonlight glinted on metal and she realized Gideon had a dagger in one hand. A low rumble sounded in his throat as the metal flicked up and into the ruffian's gut. His eyes went wide, his mouth open, and he slumped over Gideon.

Lachlan cursed and she saw him gripping his leg, blood dripping between his fingers. God forgive me, she thought, as her teeth began to chatter. The smooth wood of the handle in her palm gave her courage. She aimed at her cousin's back as he raised his broad sword over Lachlan's head. Tears blurred her vision. Her fingers squeezed the trigger. The impact of the shot sent her reeling backwards into the bush.

A yowl of pain and a curse. Alisabeth blinked, praying the bullet hit the right man. Ross screamed, the clash of steel against steel, and then Calum burst into the opening.

"What the devil is going on here?" He picked up the lifeless man by the collar and inspected his contorted face.

The crack of branches, mumbled oaths, and Ross Craigg disappeared into the darkness. Lachlan yelled, attempted to limp after the fleeing figure.

"Run ye feckin' traitor!" He grimaced and squeezed his thigh, trying to staunch the flow of blood. "Ye canna hide."

Gideon was on his knees, his breath coming out in pants. Lissie's courage fled, and she collapsed. Tears poured down her face as sobs wrenched her body. Her fingers dug into the cool earth. Then strong arms scooped her up.

"Shhh, it's over." Gideon kissed the top of her head and held her close. "I have you. You're safe now."

She clung to him, her body convulsing. "D-did I k-k-kill him?"

"Och, lass, ye just nicked him. But he'll wish ye finished him off once we find him."

Calum looked around the clearing and shook his head. "Let's get out of here and into the moonlight so we can see the damage," Calum ordered. The bedraggled group exited the copse just as Maeve and MacDunn reached the stone bench.

"God's bones," yelled Rory. "What kind of treachery is this?"

"Lissie, my poor lass, are ye all right?" Maeve's face changed from concern to horror as she took in their battered faces. "Who did this?"

Gideon groaned as he lowered himself and Alisabeth onto the bench. "That cowardly Craigg. He used Lissie to draw me into the woods."

"Why?"

He began to explain when Alisabeth peered up at his face. She gasped. "Oh, no." She gently touched his swollen eye, pulled on his bloody cravat, and used it to dab at the blood splattered across his nose and mouth. "Does it hurt?"

"Och, no. It's nothin' but a gash in my leg, needing a stitch or two or dozen. But dinna worry about me, sweet sister." Lachlan sat down heavily next to them. "I'm sure it will only fester and bleed until the surgeon has to take it off. Then ye can fetch whiskey for me and tell me what a hero I am."

Calum guffawed and bent to investigate his grandson's wound. "Ye always were a wee bit dramatic, lad. It's barely a scratch. A swallow or two of the good stuff will have ye forgetting the pain."

Peigi arrived and the cacophony of voices began again. Finally, Calum raised his hand. "We need to be getting back to the cèilidh before our guests notice. I think we should keep this to ourselves for now."

"I agree," said Peigi, after learning of the attack. "Poor Nessie and Hamish dinna need their wedding day spoiled by this. Gideon, can ye help Lachlan up the back stairs? We'll go through the kitchen."

He nodded. Alisabeth reluctantly moved off his lap, a chill going through her as she left his warm arms. "I'll clean them both up and get the cook to help sew up Lachlan's leg. She'll keep it to herself."

"We'll take turns and check on all three of ye. I'll think of an excuse for yer absence." Peigi turned to Calum. "Lissie found the wedding brought back memories of Ian and retired early. Understand?"

Calum nodded. "Lachlan and Gideon have become fast friends and fell in the whiskey barrel. They'll be dead 'til morning."

"I thank ye, all of ye," said Rory. "Ye're a good mon, Calum MacNaughton, with good kin."

The disheveled group slowly made their way around the edge of the garden. Maeve and MacDunn rejoined the festivities. Peigi handed Alisabeth a lantern. "Call for me if ye need anything, lass."

Lachlan led them through the back passage of the old keep. "I'm glad Lissie is going to England. With Ross Craigg on the loose, I'd be worried for her."

She stopped at the bottom stair and looked over her shoulder. "What? England?"

Her brother-in-law's blue eyes went wide. "Now I've gone and done it."

"Done what?" Her hands shook with anger. "Who has been making plans for me without my knowledge?"

"Mama planned to ask you tomorrow. She wants company for the winter and thought you might enjoy a change." Gideon held up his hands. "She only checked with Grandfather to be certain there were no objections before she asked you."

Lissie took a deep breath. England. She'd always imagined traveling and had grown close to Maeve. Perhaps a change would be good for her. With Lachlan leaning heavily on Gideon, she turned and led them up the stairs.

"I think it's best if we go to Lachlan's room to keep rumors at bay if we are discovered," Gideon requested as they arrived at the top of the landing.

"But her room is right here and mine is at the end of a verra long hall." Lachlan's slurred words betrayed his weakening state after the narrow stairs, his face a sickly white.

"Humor me, please, when I worry about Lissie's reputation. It's ingrained in the English." His lips quirked up in a smile as they arrived at a landing. "I can throw you over my shoulder and carry you the rest of the way."

"Over my dead body." With that, he crumpled in Gideon's grip.

Alisabeth hurried to prop a limp arm over her shoulder. Together, they half carried, half dragged the unconscious

Scot down the hall. "He's lost much blood. I hope Calum finds Enid soon. She's stitched up more gashes than rats in Edinburgh. Once she's finished, I'll make a honey poultice to keep out any infection."

By the time they reached the door, Lissie was sweating. Her brother-in-law was not a small man, though she was no weakling. They propped him on the edge of his bed then pulled him onto the mattress. A sheen of sweat covered his pale skin, and he mumbled incoherent words. Except one. Fenella.

"Who is Fenella?" Gideon sat heavily on the edge of the bed, rubbing the back of his neck. "Blasted head is killing me."

"I can give ye something for the head, but I've no idea who the woman is. Ye can wager I'll find out once he's lucid." She smiled in anticipation of that subject. "It's not a familiar name around these parts, so she must be from Glasgow."

"I'm just relieved you are not seriously harmed." He brushed the hair back from her face and gently laid it across her shoulder. She shuddered. "It's the first moment of true panic I've ever experienced."

She reached out and explored his swollen eye with a gentle finger. He grimaced and she snatched her hand back. But not before he caught it in his own. "Ye saved my life. I'm sorry for the battle scars we'll be carrying for a while. My cousin is a despicable man."

"If you come to England, I'll protect you with my life." He kissed her palm, rolled up her fingers, and held her fist against his chest. "And I swear to you, I'll be a proper gentleman. I promise to give you all the time you need to mourn. When you are ready, I will be waiting."

"And if I'm never ready?" She bit her trembling lip. His clear indigo eyes stole her breath and created odd stirrings in her belly.

"Then I'll work harder for your affections, but I'll never pressure you. I want you to be happy, Lissie. I'll do everything in my power to make that happen, whether it ends with me or another."

Her fingers traced his smooth, strong jawline. "I'll hold ye to that."

"These fool men always stirrin' up trouble." Enid bustled into the room, a bag clutched in her plump hand, and her frizzy gray curls clinging to her round cheeks. She stopped with her hand on her heaving chest. "As soon as I catch my breath, we'll begin. Tell me ye've the stomach for a little blood, my lord, for I'll need yer help to hold the ox down."

CHAPTER NINE

ONCE UPON A WIDOW©

"Men are what their mothers made them."

— RALPH WALDO EMERSON

---

*A*lisabeth woke with an aching head. She cringed as her tongue tentatively ran over her split lip. It had been a terrible night, yet a painful smile curved her lips. Throwing back the covers, her toes snuggled into the soft fur rug on the stone floor. She'd avoided any reflection of herself last night and was afraid to look in the mirror this morning.

The cèilidh had continued long into the night. A grand gathering thrown by the MacNaughtons came once, maybe twice a year, and the villagers took full advantage of the festivities, food, and drink. No one had questioned Peigi's excuses for their absence. Alisabeth hurried to dress. Her stomach growled with hunger.

The water in the basin was cold and rejuvenated her tired face. The right side of her mouth was swollen and the top lip split open. If she withstood the discomfort and pressed her lips together, it didn't look too horrible. She gingerly scrubbed her teeth, the new boar bristles rough against the inside of her bruised mouth. Then she brushed her hair and donned a fresh chemise, deep violet bodice, and skirt.

The main hall had been set up with food for anyone spending the night. It wasn't unusual to find leftover guests after a cèilidh, and especially after a wedding. Peigi had arranged for a private breakfast in the sitting room to avoid prying eyes and questions. On the way, Alisabeth stopped in to check on Lachlan. He was propped up against a mountain of pillows, his broad chest bare, and a sheet pulled up to his stomach. His auburn waves clung to his neck and shoulders, his skin shiny with sweat. He opened his deep blue eyes and grinned.

"My leg's intact, darlin', but I'll still need ye to fetch the whiskey."

"Och, you are hopeless." Relief swept through her at the sound of his cheerful voice. "Ye were half delirious when Enid pushed me out the door. I was worried the fever would take ye during the night."

"I'm not ready to raid the neighbor's pasture, but I'm better than I was." He held out a hand. "Come and sit with me, sweet Lissie. I've missed ye."

"I'm sorry my cousin has brought these troubles on the MacNaughtons." She settled next to him on the soft mattress and laced her fingers with his. Tears of embarrassment and regret stung the back of her eyes. "How is yer wound?"

"I've had the best care. No one wields a needle better than Enid. Yer poultice will keep away infection. I'll be up in no time." He pulled back the sheet to show her the bandage above his knee and wiggled his toes. Pink stained through the linen wrapped around his muscled thigh. "And no apologies for that rancid cousin. There's at least one in every clan. Ye canna blame yerself."

Alisabeth nodded, not trusting her voice.

"When will ye be leaving?"

"Do ye think I should go to England?" Her gaze locked on him. "How will I wake up each morning without this family around me?"

"Aunt Maeve will be there. She loves ye now like we do, I see it in her eyes. Ye willna be lonely." His thumb rubbed the side of her hand in comfort. "And Gideon will be there to take care of ye. He's a man of his word."

She searched his eyes for any trace of resentment but found only sympathy and affection. It had been an awkward yet healing month until last night.

"Lissie, life takes unexpected turns. We must be ready to snatch happiness in a moment because it may be our last."

"But I would never—"

He held up his other hand. "I'm only saying we love ye, lass. Death can come in the blink of an eye. If ye have the chance for some joy, take it. No one will think the worse of ye for it. Do ye understand?"

She nodded and sniffed.

"Good. Now find me a bottle of whiskey to keep me company and some of those fat, buttery biscuits ye baked."

***

Gideon licked the remnants of ham from his fingers and cursed as salt seeped into his raw knuckles. A swollen face wasn't unusual after a match at Gentleman Jackson's, but he hadn't fought without boxing gloves since university, and then only during drunken brawls.

"My poor boy," his mother crooned as she entered the small sitting room. "Your face looks worse than it did last night."

"Wait until the green and yellow replace the black and

blue. However, I can open this eye today so I'm counting my blessings." He accepted a kiss on the cheek. "I'm glad you're here before Alisabeth. I'm afraid she knows about our plans to bring her home. Lachlan mentioned it."

"And is she amenable?" Maeve poured tea and refilled his cup.

"Livid is a better word. She's proof all Scots have a temper." He chuckled when his mother opened her mouth to argue. "I think with her cousin in hiding, she'll see the wisdom in it. And she's fond of you, Mama."

"I'm verra fond of her." She scooped up soft butter from a bowl, lathered it over a biscuit, and chewed thoughtfully. "The man is a lunatic to think he could get away with murder right under our noses. His poor wife. She must be mortified."

"Or relieved that he's gone." Alisabeth stood at the door, dressed simply with her thick umber waves pulled back with a pretty ribbon. He recognized the remorse in her eyes as she scanned his face. "Does it hurt?"

"Only if I wink at pretty ladies."

"I do believe my son is acquiring a sense of humor. Thank ye, Lissie." His mother chortled. "So, my dear, will ye be joining us for the winter?"

They were both surprised at her immediate response. "I will if ye'll still have me."

Gideon watched her walk to the sideboard and ladle some porridge into a bowl. He wanted to howl and kiss her sweet swollen mouth. Maybe he had inherited more than just his grandfather's physical traits.

"Excellent. It will be a blessing for me to have the company." Maeve sighed. "I didn't realize how much I missed female companionship until my girls married and left."

"We plan on departing the day after tomorrow. Will that give you enough time? We can delay a few days, but Grandfather feels we shouldn't dally." Gideon didn't want to rush her into a decision and regret it once in England.

"I dinna have much to bring. I've told my parents and will be able to say my farewells before they leave." She hesitated. "I'm afraid I willna be dressed as well as the ladies in England. I dinna want to embarrass ye, but I've had no need of fineries here at MacNaughton Castle."

Maeve beamed. "It will be my pleasure to take ye shopping in London. My dressmaker will be delighted to have such a beautiful customer."

"Do ye think I should wear my mourning veil while we travel? There may be questions when people see the condition of our faces." Alisabeth smirked. "They'll be saying Gideon got worse than he gave."

He let out a loud guffaw, happy to see her humor back. "Just until we reach Glasgow. Lachlan wants me to check on the mill since he'll be delayed. I arranged for my solicitor to purchase a townhouse there, so we'll have only staff to worry about. Your lip should be quite healed by then."

***

Gideon was determined to keep his promise and maintain a respectable distance from Lissie. He preferred to ride anyway and knew his mother would enjoy the female conversation. She would educate her new companion on London society and the best ways to navigate the treacherous maze of the beau monde.

As the hours then days passed and the Highlands faded behind them, a melancholy overtook him. A part of him did belong to this land. His stomach knotted as he wondered how this trip, and all he learned, would affect his future. But he'd enjoyed his time in Scotland and promised Mama a return visit. Would Lissie be eager to go back or come to love Stanfeld Manor as he did? Only time would tell.

The sight of Glasgow in the distance cheered him. A

comfortable bed, good food, and excellent brandy should be waiting for them. They entered the city, and his mother poked her head out of the carriage. The groom sitting in the rear box smiled and shook his head. The servants were used to the countess' unusual ways. It was late morning and the city was bustling.

It had been several years since he'd visited. He was surprised and pleased at the growth. New streets had been added, accommodating thriving businesses. People crowded the main thoroughfares and alleyways. As they made their way to the residential area, they came upon new housing under construction. Investments were prime, and it seemed business-minded men were getting in on the boom. The once small town of Glasgow would soon challenge Edinburgh in commerce and population.

The three-story townhouse of red brick overlooked the fashionable west-end neighborhood. Gideon had sent one of the liverymen ahead to warn the staff of their arrival. A butler and housemaid opened the front door and two grooms waited on the steps. Dismounting, he tossed his reins to one of the boys and watched as the ladies exited the carriage.

His mother shaded her eyes with one hand and peered up. "So this is our new house?"

"Yes, I hope you approve. Shall we go in?" Gideon inclined his head to the staff and made introductions. Maeve began giving orders and Gideon extended his arm to Alisabeth. "Have you been to Glasgow before?"

"I've never been more than twenty-five miles from my home or MacNaughton Castle. There are so many people and carriages and horses." She shook her head. "I think it's verra grand for a visit, but I prefer the countryside."

"I can only imagine what you'll think of London." Inside the entryway, staff took their hats and coats while servants began unloading baggage. "We'll be here a couple days and then continue our journey. Would you like to visit the mill with me? I'm sure Mama will not let me out the door without her."

"I would love to see it. I've also read the new Botanic Gardens are beautiful."

"Then I will be certain you do not miss it."

***

The carriage wound its way through the city streets toward the great Clive River, stopping in front of a huge warehouse. It was Alisabeth's first look at the MacNaughton Textile Company. The dreary building, tinged with smoke and age, resembled more of a prison on the outside. Inside it was a hectic production. Two rows of power looms filled the huge space with mostly men manning the machines. Older children scurried in the aisles carrying buckets or baskets of bobbins. Lissie had only seen weaving done by hand, and marveled at the speed of the looms. The compact steel frames glinted in the sunlight pouring in from the large floor windows, their deafening mechanical *clickety-clack* drowning out any conversation by the employees.

"Welcome! It's good to see ye again, lass," boomed a voice over the machinery. Colin, one of the weavers who had brought Ian's body home, waited while Alisabeth made introductions. After explaining how the looms worked, he held out his arms and shooed them down the aisle. "This side of the factory is the wool shed, with two other sections for cotton and flax."

Alisabeth noticed several very young boys fetching items for the adults or standing by the shuttles, ready to replace the wefts with more thread. "Those wee ones canna be more than six or seven years old," she murmured to Maeve as they entered a hallway. Colin shut a thick oak door, muffling the clamor of the workroom.

The older woman's eyes narrowed as she questioned the supervisor. "Ye employ such wee ones?"

Colin nodded to Maeve and pushed a roughened hand through his silver-streaked hair. "Families need the income, my lady. Contrary to the last supervisor, I make sure they're in positions that willna cause them harm. There are enough accidents in the workplace without adding a child's death to my conscience."

They proceeded up a flight of stairs and another large room. Rows of handlooms filled the space and all the workers were women. "They used to do the weaving at home, but it's cheaper to have them here. We get a solid day's work and higher productivity, and they receive a steady income."

The back of the warehouse was filled with bolts of cloth. "Before you leave, I'd like to discuss expanding into silk. It's extremely profitable…"

Lissie wandered away from the conversation and over to a dusty window, wiped at it with the side of her fist, and peered out. Below to her left, a ship bobbed in the choppy waves of the Clyde. Workers loaded crates and bags onto carts and wheeled them off the dock. To her right, she could see part of the giant water wheel, churning the river to produce the energy needed for production. It was so much more fascinating to see the process rather than read or be told about it.

Alisabeth vaguely heard Gideon retelling the events that led to Lachlan's injury and felt three pairs of eyes on her when she turned from the window. One drop of sympathy would be too much. She was tired of pity and wanted to put it behind her. Instead, the tall Scot grinned at her.

Relief swept over her and she replied tartly, "He tells ye I almost get my throat cut and ye're laughing? I hate to think what we need to do to make ye cry, mon."

"The image of Alisabeth Craigg, brandishing a gun like a highwayman, will be stuck in my head for a week. Ye do us proud, lass. I'm sorry to have missed it." He winked at her. "They dinna enjoy the same adventures down here in the Lowlands. Too much like the English, ye ken."

"I feel I should take offense to that," laughed Gideon. "It was quite an evening. I'll admit it stirred my blood." His gaze caught hers, sharing a memory between them that warmed her. "I seem to be more my mother's son than I realized."

"I hate knowing the scoundrel is out there," Maeve said. "If they find him, he'll be on the end of rope or a boat to the penal colonies."

"Shall we go down to the office?" Colin asked. "I can show ye the accounts and last year's profits. Our bookkeeper is quite good and she already has an estimate for the rest of this year's income." His pride in the factory brought a smile to her lips. The man knew his job and worked hard.

"She?" asked Maeve. "Ye have a woman working on the books?"

"Aye, Miss Franklin is a quandary." He shook his head. "She can figure numbers in her head quicker than a spider spins a web."

The office was large with a chipped walnut desk and several mismatching chairs. One wall held shelves lined with books on textiles, weaving, and dyes. There were texts filled with illustrations of different types of machinery and others with various cloth samples. She and Maeve flipped through the squares of linen, cotton, and wool fabric as the men looked over the accounts.

"Lachlan will be another few weeks, but it seems you have everything in order. Well done, sir." Gideon shook the supervisor's hand.

"May I take some samples with me?" asked Maeve. "I plan

on making some changes at the townhouse my son purchased."

"Of course. Let me know what ye like, and I'll arrange for the locals to take care of any work ye decide to do."

The ladies tied their hats on as they prepared to leave. A pretty young woman with pale blonde hair and soft gray eyes knocked at the office entrance. "Fenella, I'm just seeing the owners out. I'll be with ye in a moment." She nodded and retreated from the doorway.

Alisabeth studied the woman as they passed, searching her memory for that name. Climbing into the carriage, she snapped her finger. "That's it!"

"That's what?" asked Gideon.

"Remember when Lachlan was incoherent with fever? He called out the name Fenella several times." She tapped her lip. "I wonder…"

Maeve laughed. "There may be more than one Fenella in Scotland, my dear. Are ye matchmaking?"

"I have a hunch there's been a match already."

She and Gideon exchanged a look then a grin. So Lachlan's mystery woman was a clerk for the MacNaughtons. And a pretty one at that.

They enjoyed a quiet meal at the townhouse that evening. Maeve asked Lissie's opinion of fabrics and other changes to the townhouse. "I hope to spend more time here. It's a perfect halfway point for my parents when I canna go all the way home."

During the next two days, Gideon met with Colin and learned more of the "dull" aspects of the MacNaughton Textiles, as he put it. He also took her and Maeve to the Botanic Gardens as promised. The last day, Colin arrived and the foursome went to Glasgow Green. It was a beautiful park, renovated after the war to provide hundreds of jobs for the unemployed. Traveling actors had set up a *geggy*, and small boys crisscrossed through the crowd announcing the showtime. The large wood frame covered with canvas would hold a large crowd.

"Are you interested in watching the performance?" asked Gideon. "I realize this may come as a surprise, but I enjoy comedies."

Alisabeth giggled. "Then ye'll be disappointed. These troupes act out Scotland's great stories and portray our most tragic historical figures." She took his arm, following Colin and Maeve into the tent. "So ye'll enjoy it even more, I'm certain."

However, the opening act had everyone laughing as a man in a short kilt attempted to play the bagpipes and dance a jig at the same time. He slipped, fell onto his side, his legs still pumping to the beat and never missing a note. He followed the act with a melancholy ballad describing the rise and fall of William Wallace. A pretty young girl of around twelve joined him to sing the lyrics and left half the crowd wiping away a tear.

That evening, Maeve kissed her son's cheek and retired, leaving them alone in the library. Gideon sipped brandy and they both sat in comfortable silence, gazes and thoughts lost in the crackling fire.

His voice startled her after the long quiet spell. "Are you enjoying yourself so far?"

"Aye, verra much. I enjoy seeing the world outside my childhood home." She smiled. "As a girl, I dreamt of becoming a pirate and sailing around the world. Silly, I know."

"My father would agree with you. And at one time, I may have also. But my views seem to be shifting in my old age."

He gave her a wicked smile. "I believe you may be the culprit behind my change of heart."

"So I should become a pirate and raid ships and collect booty?"

"I believe you are an intelligent and clever woman, who is capable of anything she sets her mind to. And I hope I'm around to see you accomplish whatever that may be, sweet Lissie." His blue eyes sparkled with warmth and affection but when he spoke her name, they darkened to midnight blue.

As she closed her eyes that night, his voice whispered to her. *Sweet Lissie.* It caressed her skin, enveloped her until she felt safe and protected and drifted into a dreamless sleep. *Sweet Lissie.*

CHAPTER TEN

"He that climbs the tall tree has won right to the fruit, he that leaps the wide gulf should prevail in his suit."

— SIR WALTER SCOTT

Late October
Stanfeld Manor

*H*is heart swelled as Alisabeth gazed upon Stanfeld Manor. She and Gideon had ridden to his favorite hilltop, overlooking the property and the best view of the house. It had been two weeks since they'd returned to England. Two weeks of walks and rides and evenings full of lively and intelligent conversation. Two weeks of getting to know Lissie, and through her, a side of his mother he'd never known. Two weeks of pure joy and pure torment. He'd give his title to make the earth stop turning, to suspend this time with the woman who was becoming more dear to him than life itself. Yet soon the world would crash in on their idyllic sanctuary. His sister arrived at the end of the week, and the dressmaker would call in the morning.

Strangers might create tension, cause her smile to falter or her confidence to waver. Gideon didn't want anything to break the fragile bond he'd worked so hard to forge. He had watched Alisabeth bloom like a winter rose, peeking out at first, testing the air, and then spreading those glorious petals. She filled his neat and tidy world with color he hadn't realized was lacking. In return, she trusted him to introduce her to new things, new adventures without condescension. His arrogance vanished in her presence.

"It is the opposite of MacNaughton Castle, so fairytale-like. Each time I cross that bridge, I feel as if I'm a princess entering my royal courtyard." She smiled at him, those honey eyes warm and soft. "I can see why ye are so proud of it."

"Ah, that is where we differ. I do love this place. It's my childhood home. But there is something steady and dependable, practical really, that draws me to Grandfather's keep." He enjoyed these discussions. Her opinions were thoughtful and often revealed another irresistible layer of her personality. "Perhaps it's what the place symbolizes—centuries of survival and family. So much history imbedded in that stone."

"And voices demanding to be heard still whisper in those walls, if ye take the time to listen. Unhappy souls needing their stories told so they may be at peace." She tilted her head and eyed him thoughtfully. "Do ye believe in such things?"

"I really don't know anymore. The last months have taught me that things are not always what they seem." He shrugged. "Mama says an open mind would serve me well. Yet it's hard to ignore the foundation on which you were raised."

"Aren't we the philosophical ones so early in the day?" Lissie pulled lightly on the reins, squeezed the mare's sides, and expertly turned the horse on its hindquarters to face him. She gave him a brilliant smile. "I'll race ye down the hill and to that *modern* bridge. Ready, set—"

Little Bit, his tail in the air and his paws digging furiously at something under a large oak, stopped at the familiar words and joined the pair. Gideon chuckled. "He thinks he can win, you know. I must admit the mongrel is surprisingly fast for his size. Do you miss the deerhounds?"

"Terribly, though this wee scruff is a fine substitute. And he fits on my lap, which was never an option with Brownie or Black Angus." Her eyes went wide, and her mouth made an "O."

"And when was Little Bit on your lap?" The dog slept in the barn and wasn't allowed inside. At least, not before the arrival of one dark-haired, golden-eyed Scot.

"Weel, I *may* have let him sneak past Sanders once or twice. And I *may* have let him keep me company while ye were out with yer steward, and yer ma was busy with correspondence." Her eyes sparkled with mischief, her long slender finger tapping her full lips as if in concentration. "But I canna say for sure."

Gideon laughed and shook his head. "You have a short memory for one so young. I'll be surprised if you can remember your name by next year."

The dog barked, his tail wagging so fast Gideon almost felt a breeze. "Fine, we'll race. Ready, set,"—he kicked Verity and bolted ahead—"go!"

"Ah, the devil take ye and yer cheatin' ways," she cried from behind him.

The two horses galloped down the hill and raced across the field. Both took the hedge without issue, but as they neared the bridge, Gideon heard a scream. His heart plunged into his stomach, and he pulled Verity up. Lissie and her mare flew past him, laughter drifting behind her. With a curse and a reluctant grin, he clucked to the gelding and caught up to the girl and the dog waiting under the yew tree.

"Two can play at that game, my lord," she chortled as he tried to look indignant. "Never underestimate yer opponent. Calum taught me that."

"Wise words I should heed." He bowed, thinking how delectable she looked in his mother's riding habit. She drew in deep breaths, and the forest green jacket and skirt that hugged her curves accentuated her heaving chest. Gideon pulled his gaze back to her face, as he had been careful to do every day since he'd made the decision to marry her. "Even the dog beat me!"

He dismounted then moved to help her down. Before he could reach her, Alisabeth flipped her leg over the saddle and slid to the ground with her backside to him. *Good God, this will be a long six months*, he thought with a grin and a grimace. That was the earliest he could begin a courtship, and he hoped to have already won her affection. After that, he'd woo her until he captured her heart. Until then, he would remain a perfect gentleman if it killed him.

The horses bent their necks and munched greedily on the last of the summer grass. "Why does yer ma think I need so many dresses? I canna wear more than one at a time. Three or four should be more than enough."

"Ah, my dear girl. If you were in London, you would need a morning dress, an afternoon dress, and of course ball dresses. And a chit cannot wear the same dress in the same company. In the country, and since you are in mourning, your entertainment is limited." He paused, cursing himself when he saw a momentary shadow cross her face. "Our social schedule will be limited to local guests and small dinner parties. *Perhaps*, if you are *very* well behaved, some dancing. We do not have to follow protocol to the letter if there's no one to witness our impropriety."

The light was back in her smile, and the heaviness in his chest eased.

"There is always a darker side to every cloud, I suppose. And is throwing propriety to the wind part of yer new open-mindedness?"

"Perhaps. Along with the opportunity to teach a beautiful woman how to waltz. It's a very romantic dance." He wiggled his eyebrows, trying to keep the tone light. His body was quickly responding to the thought of holding her close.

"I look forward to the lesson, my lord." She pointed to a carriage parked in the courtyard. "We have guests. It's quite fancy for a dressmaker. But if she makes such extensive wardrobes for all the girls coming out, I imagine she's quite *plump in the pocket*." She added her best English accent to the last bit of cant.

Gideon chuckled. Her imitation of an English noble was quite good. The woman had a knack at mockery that made one guffaw rather than glare. Perhaps it was her ability to laugh at herself that endeared her to everyone. The servants adored her, and she'd already charmed her way into the kitchen. Even his stodgy butler Sanders seemed smitten with her, a crooked smile on his face whenever she cast a smile his way.

They walked across the bridge, the clatter of hooves echoing in the quiet morning air. He studied the conveyance. "That's the Marlen crest. Marietta has arrived early." *She probably ordered the carriage as soon as she got the letter*, he thought with a grin. His mother must have mentioned their guest and his interest in her.

Lissie slowed her step. "Does she know about…everything?"

"Mama wrote her and told her of our trip. But I'm sure

she'll have plenty of questions so she can fend off the *on-dits* when she's in London. Rumors have a way of slinking into the parlors and ballrooms of that city." He winked at her. "Should we give them something to gossip about?"

"Ye are incorrigible, Gideon. I'm anxious to meet yer sister now and see who she takes after. It sounds like yer ma, or at least I'm hoping." She grinned. "Ye may be sorely outnumbered with opinions when we gather around the hearth tonight."

"Nothing would please me more." To his surprise, he meant it. He handed off the horses to the stable boy. Lissie thanked the groom who had followed them as a chaperone. No one and no deed escaped her notice.

Sanders greeted them at the door. Alisabeth stood on her tiptoes, placed her hand on his shoulder, and whispered something in his ear. He nodded, turned a bright red, and mumbled, "Any time, my lady." Then to Gideon, "My lord, Lady Marlen has arrived. She and the countess are having breakfast in the dining room."

His stomach growled at the mention of food, and he pushed Lissie down the hall. "Are you flirting with my butler?"

"I only thanked him for the advice he's given me. I dinna ken the intricacies of yer world, and he's been verra kind to guide me." She gave him a side look as they entered the room. "I'm determined not to embarrass ye when visitors come calling."

"You are delightful, my dear, and would never be an embarrassment," replied his mother from the long table. She and Marietta stood and Gideon made the introductions.

Etta's sharp eyes surveyed the widow, and then she held out her hand with a warm smile. "It is a pleasure to meet you. Mama's letter had me intrigued." She glanced at Gideon with a smirk as she perused Alisabeth. "She *is* a beauty."

Lissie blushed and thanked her. "And ye take after yer mother, I see, not afraid to speak yer mind. I was hoping as much."

Etta's profile in an emerald green dress showed a rounding belly, the white satin ribbon emphasizing the bump. "I hope I didn't irritate you, Gideon, when I changed my plans. I know you don't like last minute changes, but if I waited too long, Bradford—that's my husband, Viscount Marlen," she explained to Lissie, "would not have let me come. He has secured the best physicians for the birthing. No country doctors for his first child."

"The babe is expected in February?" Gideon didn't like the thought of any of his sisters in childbirth. Too many infants and women died in the process. Though his mother had survived labor seven times, only four had survived. "I will do my best to get Mama to London."

"I know you will." Etta patted his cheek and then ignored him. "Do you want to change before the interrogation begins? Or would you prefer some porridge and biscuits to bolster your strength so we can get started right away? I want to know all about you and Scotland and…"

His sister linked arms with Lissie, and they moved to the table. Gideon thought of his grandfather's scotch and wondered if he'd need his own fortitude bolstered to withstand the barrage of females.

***

Alisabeth realized her worries had been for naught. Etta was as warm and open as Maeve. She was also full of energy and never seemed to stop moving, even in her condition. Embroidery held her attention a scant fifteen minutes. When she moved on to a book or pastels, her foot tamped as if her mind was already thinking about what to tackle next. There was no instrument in the music room Marietta had not mastered. Accomplished did not begin to describe her.

"Those talents are due to her inability to sit still," Maeve said one night after Etta had played the violin, the harp, and the pianoforte. "My daughter must be busy all the time. She inherited her father's stubbornness and never ceases until she's mastered whatever is her latest fancy."

"I do believe you're in possession of that tenacious quality yourself, dear Mama," Gideon said as he leaned down to kiss her cheek. He grinned at the nasty look she cast him in reward.

She and Gideon's sister had become fast friends after a week. The family had gathered in the drawing room again, enjoying a light melody by Etta on the lute. Rain splattered the windowpanes, and an occasional streak of lightning added a flash of light upon the room.

"Whoever was responsible for my single-mindedness, it certainly came in handy when I pursued my husband." She positioned her fingers again on the strings of the lute and played a little more.

"An unfair match to be sure. The poor sot never stood a chance. Once Etta decided Marlen would be her husband, she was relentless. She was at every event he attended, wearing her most seductive gowns, tripping in front of him, spilling champagne down his waistcoat..." Gideon put his hand to one side of his mouth and whispered loudly, "I think he realized it was easier to give in than to fight her."

Lissie pressed her lips together as Etta continued to play but softly snuck up behind her brother. She loved watching their good-natured teasing.

Thump! "Ouch!" Gideon rubbed his head.

"He succumbed to my feminine charms, you dolt." She reached up and twisted the hairs at his nape, the gold specks in her light brown eyes flashing. "Admit it." She yanked and his head tipped back.

"Fine, your exquisite manners won him over," he said

with gritted teeth but winked at Lissie. When Etta let go, he jibed, "And that is an example of her infamous charm!"

"Children, children," called Maeve in mock severity. "I shall send you to your rooms. Gideon, why don't you sing?"

"I think Etta should sing. That would chase the devil from his den."

His sister confided to Alisabeth. "I'm the only one in the family who cannot sing. I sound like a sheep giving birth in a blizzard."

"And how many sheep have ye witnessed giving birth in a blizzard?" Lissie quipped.

"Touché," said Gideon, an appreciative gleam in his eye.

"It was a stormy winter's night when I helped Brownie and Black Angus into the world." She explained to Marietta, "They're yer grandfather's favorite dogs—Scottish deerhounds."

"What odd names," she remarked. "One sounds as if it belongs to a smaller dog and the other to a highwayman."

Alisabeth laughed. "They're faeries, ye ken. One is sweet and the other is Death."

"Come sit by the fire and tell them about our Scottish faeries." Maeve patted the cushion next to her on the settee. "I want my grandchildren to know all of our history."

Lissie sat next to her and smoothed out the sienna lace covering the muslin of her new gown. Maeve had remarked how it set off her cognac eyes. Well, how best to begin with an audience who had no knowledge of them? "The Wee Folk have been part of Scotland since time began. There are both benevolent and dangerous faeries so they're not creatures to call up on a whim."

Her audience nodded and assumed a more serious expression while Maeve chuckled at the reprimand.

"Our girl Brownie is like her namesakes, the sweetest, kindest of all the faeries. Odd little dwarves with shiny black eyes, pointed ears, and long fingers. They canna stand liars, cheats, misers, or cats."

"Cats?" asked Etta, her brow arched as her fingers drummed the armrest.

"They hate cats, drink milk and ale, and love honey and cake. If you think a Brownie has come upon yer house, check the attic or cellar."

"How would you know?"

"They look for homes filled with deserving folk and help with chores around the house. So ye'll go to chop the wood or draw water from the well and find it already done. Verra helpful, they are."

"So what about Black Angus?" Gideon leaned forward on the leather chair, his elbows on his knees and his chin resting on a fist. "Since I've met the hound, Death sounds appropriate."

"He warmed up to ye after a time. In our tongue, he's *Cu Sith*, which translates to faerie dog, a huge black hound with golden eyes and sharp teeth. It is said that anyone confronted by him will die within two weeks' time. He jumps in your path and growls his message of death before slinking away." Lissie lowered her voice conspiratorially, "Calum says his great-great grandfather named a deerhound Black Angus from every litter. Anytime an Englishman came close to the property, he'd send his dog of death to greet them."

"And did they die?" asked Etta.

She shrugged. "The English were never invited to stay, ye ken. The MacNaughtons continued the custom. Calum, as his father before him, uses each Black Angus as a guard dog. No one wants the hound sitting in front of him and growling, so they stay verra quiet and dinna move."

"So that's why he put the dog next to Ross when we were in the village." Gideon grinned. "If he put up a fuss or ran, the dog would block him, and he might be cursed."

Maeve stifled a yawn. "Thank ye, Lissie, for sharing with us. Perhaps we can hear more tomorrow night?"

"Whenever ye like, my lady." She squeezed the older lady's hand. "I thank ye, all of ye, for making me feel so welcome."

Marietta jumped up and hugged her. "I'm so glad to have met you. Our time together is much too short. You must promise to come with Mama when the babe is born."

"If Maeve will have me, I'd love to meet the bairn and your husband. But ye dinna leave until next week, so let's not think of parting yet."

That night as Lissie prepared for bed, she thought of Scotland and her family and the faeries. Wistfulness assailed her, and she wiped away a tear from her cheek as she peered out the window. If only she had a bit of home, she thought as she made out the blurred image of a willow tree through the slanting rain. A dim light flickered in its branches at the same time she heard a faint sound. A beautiful voice humming a sweet, compelling melody.

Lissie ran to the door and looked up and down the hall. Saints and sinners, nothing in the passageway. She went back to the window. The light flickered again and then went out. The faerie voice faded away. Her heart lifted inexplicably, and the homesickness in her soul eased.

CHAPTER ELEVEN

"Friendship may, and often does, grow into love, but love never subsides into friendship."

— LORD BYRON

Stanfeld Estate
February 1820

Gideon tied his cravat with deft fingers, adjusted the small diamond pin, and inspected his reflection. The cranberry waistcoat and dark blue tailcoat were expertly tailored. He was complete to a shade—even he would want to court this image in the mirror, he thought wryly. But Alisabeth's approval was all that mattered. He would ask her tonight after supper, during a game of chess. The board would keep a barrier between them so he wouldn't be tempted to kiss those plump, pink lips.

They had grown close over the last months, and he had

slowly begun to appreciate her unusual views and astute observations. Not only was she beautiful, she was awake on every suit, clever with a discerning mind. At first, he had been concerned their different upbringings would be a hindrance, but it was the opposite. She opened his mind to possibilities he had never imagined. With some surprise, Gideon realized he valued her opinion.

Birks had received an offer last week to lease a large section of land. The terms were generous and the tenants' terms would be up at the end of the year. He had brought up the subject at dinner, and Lissie had offered her thoughts. If the tenants could afford a higher rent, or offered a percentage of their yield, Gideon would not have to evict families who had been on the estate for generations. Her reasoning made sense. The tenants rotated crops among themselves, keeping the soil rich. A large lease would drain the acreage for a quick and hefty income, but the land would yield little after the lease was up.

In the end, Gideon had turned down the short-term profit for a long-term investment with his tenants. Yes, Alisabeth would make an excellent match for him, and he could not imagine a life without her. Her smile when he entered the room, and the light in her eyes when they brushed against one another, told him she must feel the same. Yet, worry niggled at him.

The trio had managed a trip to Glasgow before Christmas since the weather had been mild. His grandparents had come without his aunt's family but, to Lissie's delight, had brought the Craiggs. Glynis had been recuperating from a fever, and his cousin Brodie had not wanted her to travel. They had all been delighted to see family again. Gideon had welcomed the opportunity for his future in-laws to get know him better without the pressure of a betrothal.

Lachlan was fully recovered and back at the mill, overseeing all exports, imports, and production. Colin had been assigned overseer of all employees. Romance, it seemed, had been flitting about MacNaughton Textile. Lachlan was now married to the mystery woman, Fenella, though it had been a rocky start. The blonde Englishwoman had not been honest about her own background. But she had been as stubborn as a Scot, using feminine wiles and short bread to win back his heart.

Colin was doggedly pursuing Fenella's friend and companion, though they learned from Lachlan that the silly girl was resisting his marriage proposal. But the man was formidable when on a mission. It seemed to be a family trait.

And I am indeed on a mission, he thought as he fiddled with the cravat again.

His mother knew what he was about and had arranged a delectable supper for that evening. He walked into the dining room and inspected the setting. Freshly polished silver sparkled in the candlelight. Mead from Ireland, Lissie's favorite, had been brought up from the cellar. It would be served with the last course, warmed with a hint of lemon.

Both women entered, chattering about the cold and the pond freezing over. Shimmering violet silk accentuated Alisabeth's soft curves beneath a delicate black lace. The overlay did not hide the creamy white mounds that beckoned his fingers to cup their round fullness. He quickly lifted his gaze to her warm smile, but the sensuous mouth did nothing to dampen his ardor. He assisted them to their seats and concentrated on his mother.

Over clear soup, he struggled for conversation, his nerves getting the best of him. "So you know the pond is frozen, Mama? We haven't been skating since before I went to university. Would you be up to it?"

"Yes, I was just thinking about Lake Perfect. We had such

marvelous times there with the family. Have ye ever been ice skating?" she asked Alisabeth.

Lissie shook her head. "No, but I'm a willing pupil if ye're a patient teacher. Lake Perfect?" she asked with a giggle. "It sounds...perfect!"

Gideon's mind envisioned the two of them on the ice, his arm around her waist, holding her up on the slippery surface. *Pay attention to the conversation, you blunderhead.* He brought his mind back to the present. "My youngest sister Helen gave it the moniker and the name stuck. It provided fishing for me, swimming for all of the siblings, skating for the entire family, and sustenance for the 'wood folk' on the property."

"Wood folk?"

"Anything living in the woods were 'folk' to Helen. As a child, she insisted she could speak to them." He chuckled. "She did have long conversations with several bullfrogs, I remember. They just never answered her back."

Lissie made a *ribbit* sound and giggled again. "So the pond offered something for everyone. What a fitting name then. Yes, I would love to visit Lake Perfect."

"Tomorrow afternoon? If the sun is shining, I'll have the groom hook up the sleigh. Mama, would the girls have left their skates here?"

"Of course. I'll have a housemaid search for them in the morning. Ice skates are not a priority in a woman's trousseau." She waited while Gideon served them sections of white fish in a cream sauce. "I may even join you. The fresh air would do me good. Your father loved the pond in winter. It was the only activity that would tempt him out on a cold day."

"That's right, he taught you how to skate." Gideon and his sisters had been given wooden platforms with blades when they were old enough to stand without wobbling. "He always worried one of us would catch a chill. After an hour, hot bricks and spiced wine and cider would appear to warm us up. Then we'd set out once more."

"In Scotland if we let the cold keep us inside, we'd never leave the hearth." Lissie took a bite of the fish and wiped her mouth. "Maeve, it must have been verra hard for ye to move here alone."

The older woman considered. "It was but love seems to help ye face whatever obstacles are in the way."

Gideon listened to the women compare differences in the households. He marveled at how his mother's accent fluctuated, depending on the company. When they were alone, as now, she was Maeve from Scotland. When they entertained the neighbors, her speech was modulated and proper. A chameleon, to be sure, he thought with a smirk.

After roasted potatoes and turnips with rosemary and a glazed goose with cranberry sauce, Lissie patted her stomach. "I swear I'll look like Etta if I eat another bite. It was a wonderful meal."

Maeve beamed as she poured them a cup of the mead. The last tray arrived with a variety of sweet meats. "I'm glad ye enjoyed it. But ye must have one or two of these."

Gideon was not surprised when, a few minutes later, his mother yawned and made her excuses. He loved her for it but suddenly felt like a Johnny raw. "We will see you tomorrow, Mama. Alisabeth, a game of chess?"

"I'd love to since ye're a win ahead of me."

They settled into their usual chairs, Gideon taking his black pieces and Lissie arranging the white. She had brought a cup of warm mead with her, and he poured himself a second brandy. For courage. Why was he so blasted nervous? She reached for a pawn then paused, her teeth biting that full lower lip.

"Alisabeth, I need to speak with you about something." Did his voice quaver? *Good God, man, get hold of yourself.*

"Yes, Gideon? It sounds serious." She put the ivory piece down and gave him her full attention.

The candlelight danced on the glossy pearls at her neck, lending a radiant effect to her skin. Those gilded eyes studied him, and his mouth went dry.

"I believe we have grown close over the past months and forged a solid friendship. Would you agree?" *She is merely a woman,* his reason told him. *Just come out with it!*

"Oh yes. You have been so kind and attentive. I'm verra… content here at Stanfeld Manor." She lowered her gaze, the thick lashes creating a dark arc against her flushed cheeks. The firelight sent shadows across her exquisite face and highlighted the curve of her jaw.

He stifled a moan. "I wish to take our relationship a step further. I would like to court you, if you would not be opposed."

He recognized the panic and it sobered him. Not because she may not care for him, which would be devastating, but he would not see her unhappy at any price. If his overtures caused any sort of upset, he would abandon his pursuit of her.

"I am honored, my lord. But it's not been a year since Ian died, and I worry what—"

"Others might think?" He hadn't thought her susceptible to society gossip, one of the traits he had come to love about her. His chest tightened. "We could keep the courtship private, if you prefer."

"Och, no. Why would I care what strangers think?" She placed her fingers in his hand. "I dinna want Ian's memory clouded by anything I might do. But he was my best friend, and I fear he will always be a part of my heart."

Gideon sighed and sent up a silent prayer to his cousin. He was in love with Lissie and could not imagine any of his family begrudging them happiness. "Yet your relationship, if

I understand correctly, was more affection than desire. You did not love him the way I love you." He heard the intake of breath and knew he'd hit the mark. "I am willing to wait until you're ready. But if you do not hold any tender feelings for me, I will never press you again."

Tears sparkled in her eyes. Regret? That she had never loved Ian in that way or that she would never love *him* in that way? He pulled a handkerchief from his pocket and handed it to her.

"I apologize. I dinna usually cry." She gave him a watery smile and dabbed at her eyes. "I've come to depend on you, share my thoughts with you, spend time with you. I almost wish everything could stay just as it is now."

"I'm afraid it's too late for that. My feelings are much too strong to remain as we have been." He took a deep breath then let it out in a rush. He held her gaze, wanting to wipe the tears from her eyes and kiss those quivering lips. "What I mean to say, my sweet Lissie, is that I need to move forward. You are constantly in my head, in my dreams. I must know there is a chance for us or find a way to deal with the emptiness of a life without you." He squeezed her warm trembling fingers, reading the sadness in her eyes that now clouded his own heart.

"May I have time to consider?" He nodded and she continued tremulously, "My emotions are a muddle right now. Ye must ken ye're in my heart, but my mind says I've no right to be happy with ye. Yet it is yer kindness and...verra presence that have helped me begin to heal."

"The fact I'm in your heart is enough for now." He stood and pulled her to her feet. "Take as long as you need. You know how I feel. I can only leave the matter in your hands."

He kissed her on the cheek and his lips lingered, breathing in her faint scent of lavender, not wanting to break the contact. It might be the last time he would be this close to her. A lump formed in his throat, and he cleared it noisily. "If my declaration has made you uncomfortable, I apologize. But I will never regret falling in love with you."

***

Alisabeth went to bed, her mind whirling. He loved her. Not cared for her, felt a kinship toward her, or was fond of her but *loved* her. She'd been attracted to him the first time their eyes met, but it had been the wedding when she realized it was more than physical attraction. She'd remembered the look in the couple's eyes as they said their vows. She had never shared that kind of look with Ian, but that day she had shared it with Gideon. Since then, her conscience had battled against the desire. How could she experience the kind of passion Ian had been denied? What gave her the right to a bright future and such rhapsody? It would be disloyal to her dead husband and all he'd given up for her.

Yet she longed to know Gideon's touch, how it would feel to be held in his arms, to be kissed with passion and not just affection. Guilt knotted her stomach each time tender feelings for him rose in her chest. Lord Stanfeld was a good man and understood her. But they had led such different lives. Yet, Maeve had found happiness here in England. *Ian, ye were always there to guide me. How I need yer common sense now.*

Lissie went to her wardrobe and searched along the dark bottom. She found the hand-carved box Ian had made for her fifteenth birthday. Lifting the lid, she took out the silk gloves and breathed in the scent of home as tears fell down her cheeks. She carefully laid them under her pillow, undressed, and went to bed. Perhaps an answer would come to her in sleep. As slumber evaded her, a haunting melody wafted through her brain. The same faerie-like humming she'd heard before. The same peace that it had brought then comforted her now, and her lids grew heavy.

She awoke refreshed, anticipating the day. Gideon was not at breakfast. Lissie was both disappointed and relieved.

"Gideon said he had arrangements to make for later." Maeve studied her. "Ye look well, lass. Did ye sleep soundly?"

She nodded. "Like a babe with a bit of whiskey on its gums."

"Anything ye'd like to talk about?"

Alisabeth had the sense Maeve knew about Gideon's request. The need for a confidante overrode her embarrassment. "Oh Maeve, I dinna ken what to do. Gideon professed his love for me but I'm afraid…"

"Afraid? Of happiness?"

Lissie hesitated then nodded. "Ian and I loved each other but we were not *in* love. The emotions Gideon stirs in me—I never experienced with Ian."

"Do you think you deserve to be happy?" Maeve left her chair and sat next to her. "What would Ian want you to do?"

She shook her head. "Why should fate allow me to find the kind of passion I didna allow him to have? It wouldna be fair, ye see."

"Life is often unfair." Maeve placed a hand on Lissie's cheek. "I've come to know ye, lass, and I knew my nephew. He made his own choices and he chose you. Nothing would give him more pain than to see ye miserable."

She sniffed. "I ken that, I do, but I also canna help but wonder if I let him down…"

"*What ifs* will never help ye find answers, my sweet." Maeve smiled sadly. "I'll ask ye what my ma asked me when Charles proposed, and I was reluctant to leave my home. Can ye imagine yer life without him? It's really as simple as that."

Alisabeth pondered Maeve's words as the maid helped her dress that afternoon.

"Here, my lady. I have more petticoats for you." The girl handed her another pair of stockings as well. "Lady Stanfeld said to make sure you are warm. She won't have you taking a chill."

"I'm not sure how I will be able to move with all these layers. I already have two petticoats, stockings and wool socks." She laughed as she struggled into another petticoat and donned her chemise.

"Those were flannel, this one is lighter and will fit over the others easy enough. Frozen limbs don't move so good neither, my lady."

"I shall be sweating like a day in July."

The maid clucked, pulled a chemise over Lissie's head, and helped her into the deep blue dress. Finally, she arranged a soft wool shawl around her mistress' shoulders and tucked a pair of fingerless gloves in a pocket.

Downstairs, Maeve waited with a coat and a heavy wool cape, its hood and sleeves trimmed in red fox. A matching fur muff for her hands completed the ensemble.

"Saints and sinners! If I break through the ice, I'll fall straight to the bottom of Lake Perfect," Alisabeth laughed as the sleigh pulled up to the front door. Her breath caught when the driver turned. Gideon smiled. A sweet, patient smile full of love and hope. Her heart wrenched at the thought of causing him any pain.

He hopped down from the sleigh and handed first Maeve then Alisabeth into the seats. She avoided his eyes but could not stop the thudding of her heart. They snuggled under a large fur blanket and placed their feet on the foot warmers. "I thought I'd drive us there. Sanders has arranged for a carriage to come out in an hour or so with more hot coal. It will be a nice respite and allow us to thaw out a bit."

The drive to the pond was spectacular. It had snowed overnight again, and icicles glittered on the bare tree branches. The snow crunched beneath the horses' hooves, their harnesses jingling in steady rhythm. Puffs of white clouds floated up and away as they talked or sang. Lissie breathed in the crisp, cold air and it cleared her head.

When they reached their destination, she sighed. Lake Perfect was indeed perfect. Two wrought iron benches stood side by side next to the pond. Willow trees stood protectively at each end, the drooping bare branches heavy with glistening snow.

"Charles loved this place. It does my heart good to be here again. It brings back wonderful memories," Maeve said, longing evident in her voice. "Och, I'm getting too sentimental in my old age."

"There's nothing old about ye, Maeve." Lissie gave her a hug. "Thank ye so much for inviting me here."

"Bringing ye here to England or here to the pond?"

"Both!"

Gideon stood, a pair of wool socks stretched over his muscled calves and a deep blue great coat that added bulk to his shoulders. He tipped his hat and pulled a sack out from under the driver's seat. "Let's see what size will fit your shoes."

He helped them down from the sleigh and deposited them on one of the benches. There were several pair of wooden slats, with long blades on the bottom that curled up in front of the toes and straps on the top to fasten over her leather shoes. Maeve and Gideon quickly attached their skates before Gideon turned to help Lissie. He squatted down in front of her, laid his hand on the back of her ankle, and slid the skate under her foot. His gloved hand, on such an intimate part of her, sent her stomach tumbling. The touch lingered and again she closed her eyes, afraid to gaze into his. By the time he'd finished strapping on the other skate, Lissie had convinced herself that he could not seduce her with a look.

She pulled on her kid gloves and slapped her knees. "No

time like the present, I suppose." Holding on to the back of the bench, she rose cautiously. One step. One more step. She grinned. "It's not as difficult as I thought."

"Ye haven't even been on the ice yet, ye silly goose." Maeve laughed and took the lead. "I'll be busy enough taking care of myself. Alisabeth is your responsibility, Gideon. She's in your hands now."

"It seems you have a talent for reading minds, Mama."

CHAPTER TWELVE

"Let other pens dwell on guilt and misery."

— JANE AUSTEN

---

*T*he countess stepped onto the pond and glided across the slick surface. Alisabeth took a tentative step and gripped Gideon's arm as her foot slid out in front of her. A strong arm went around her waist, and the other hand grasped her fingers so they were side by side. *Weel*, she thought, *I'll be too busy staying upright to worry about my heart. It's my bottom that's in danger now.*

"Hold your dress up so you don't trip, and lean on me if you feel unbalanced." His deep, assuring tone calmed her nerves. "Now, we'll move left then right. Left then right."

Under his expert tutelage, she found herself sliding over the ice. The sun had come out, and the pond reflected the winter rays like a mirror. Her fists gripped the layered materials beneath her coat and Gideon's fingers. "I hope I'm not hurting ye," she squeaked, leaning precariously to one side as they made a turn around the edge.

He laughed—a carefree sound that warmed her chilled bones and made her smile. She had worried the outing might be uncomfortable after their conversation last night. Instead, being next to him, his body brushing hers as their legs sashayed back and forth, seemed natural. His hold on her was comforting and exciting at once, and for the first time that day, Lissie's shoulders eased and her muscles relaxed.

"I'm a sturdy half-Scot, don't you know? Just say the word when you're tired, and I'll whisk you back to the bench." He pulled her closed and spun her in a circle.

"Oh my, it's almost like floating. Or flying," she gasped and was rewarded with a brilliant smile from Gideon. His blue eyes absorbed the winter sun, clear and sparkling with mischief.

"Fly, you say?"

Gideon picked her up under the armpits, swung her around in an arc, and placed her back on the ice in one fluid motion. Her stomach tumbled with excitement, and she marveled at his strength and the ease in which he'd lifted her. "I thought it had been years since ye've skated?" she asked breathlessly. "I'm impressed it's come back to ye so quickly."

"You bring out the best in me."

"Stop showing off! He used to spin circles around his sister Lottie until she would wail with dizziness," countered Maeve as she glided next to them. "However, I agree. Ye do bring out the best in my son."

Lissie blushed and picked up the pace, the sharp scratch of blades against ice creating a rhythmic accompaniment to their graceful movements.

An hour passed and a carriage parked next to the sleigh. They climbed inside to warm their feet, drink mulled wine, and nibble on sweet meats. Once settled, Sanders appeared with an envelope, bearing the Marlen seal.

"I know you have been anxious for news, my lady, so I brought this along." He paused, his stoic face cracking a bit as his lips turned up ever so slightly. "We're all on tenterhooks."

Maeve slid a nail under the wax seal. "Wait a moment, Sanders." She scanned the letter, her eyes glistening. "It's a boy. A healthy boy and Etta is doing well. Please let the staff know when we return."

"It would be my pleasure, my lady," he said with a crooked smile.

"She produced the coveted heir on her first attempt, eh? Well, as long as Etta's fine." Gideon grinned. "And did the Viscount Marlen survive?"

"You're incorrigible. Of course he did." The countess tucked the letter in her muff. She turned to Alisabeth. "Are ye enjoying the afternoon?"

"I can see why this was a favorite outing," said Lissie, leaning back into the soft velvet seat. "Maeve, ye're so graceful out there. I shall try it solo when we are finished."

"I'm sure ye'll do fine. I'll be heading home after this. I'm done to a cow's thumb. It's been so long since I've skated, my legs will rebel tomorrow." She held up her spiced wine. "Here's to another outing soon."

They clinked their cups together and a short while later bid farewell to Maeve. Back on the ice, Gideon escorted her around the perimeter of the pond several more times while she found her balance again. Satisfied, he let her go.

Lissie let out a nervous laugh as she tottered then straightened with a huge smile. "I'm doing it. I'm staying up on my own." She clapped her hands and then panicked. "How do I stop?"

In a blink, Gideon was in front of her, skating backward. "Take my hands." She did and continued to move forward, following his lead. "You're very good, Alisabeth. I knew you would be."

After several times around, he slowed and came to a stop. Her blades continued and her body bumped his hard chest. Her legs slipped, and she grasped at the lapels of his great coat. His arms went around her, pulling her body flush against his. It was the most glorious sensation. A throbbing began in her belly and moved lower. She gasped at the unfamiliar response.

"I've got you. I won't let you fall."

Her breath caught as she looked up, his face so close to hers. She couldn't pry her eyes from his mouth. Without thought, she pulled on his coat, stretched up on her toes, and pressed her lips to his. They were soft and tasted of cloves and cinnamon. Her eyes closed as Gideon groaned then kissed the corners of her mouth.

"Are you sure you want to do this?" His husky voice sent a tremor through her body, and the pulsing increased low in her belly. She could only nod her head.

He moved against her, one arm holding her close. His gloved hand cupped her jaw, and they spun in a slow, sensuous circle while he teased and nibbled her top lip. It was everything she dreamed it would be. Sweet, dizzying, and never enough. She opened her mouth to him. When his tongue swept in, heat crashed through her body. Her arms went around his neck, and she hung on for dear life. Their bodies glided and swirled as one, connected like the perfect jigsaw puzzle. When he broke the kiss, he leaned his forehead against hers. His thumb lazily traced the line of her jaw.

"Does this mean yes, my darling Alisabeth?"

She tried to gain control of her senses, but the desire still jumbled her brain. The sound of her panting mixed with his, puffy clouds rising between them and connecting before floating away on the crisp, cold air. Lissie closed her eyes, searching the depths of her soul for the answer. The heaviness in her chest, with her since Ian's death, eased and the guilt receded. Her heart had decided. With a great sigh of relief, she knew it was the right choice.

She opened her eyes. Cerulean blue orbs sent another wave of heat through her core. "Yes, yes! The answer is yes."

Gideon dipped his head and covered her mouth. This time the kiss demanded her response as he caressed her back. His hard length pressed against her thigh, and the throbbing between her legs increased. She clung to him, her mind cluttered with the touch of his hands, his velvet lips. *Saints and sinners*, she thought, *how I love this man.*

***

Early March 1820
  London

Little Edward fussed and squalled at all the attention. The babe was swaddled in a plaid Maeve had brought from MacNaughton Castle, a gift from his great-grandparents. His little red face screwed up and a loud belch rang out.

"Weel, he definitely has some MacNaughton in him," laughed Maeve, rocking the child and smoothing the blonde fuzz on his tiny skull. "I wonder if his eyes will stay blue? I think I see gold specks in there."

"I can only pray he looks like his mother," said Marlen, running a hand through his unruly brown hair. "But I'd prefer my temperament for him."

"Agreed," said Etta. She kissed her brother on the cheek.

"I'm so glad you could bring them, Gideon, even if it's only for a short while."

"My pleasure," he said with a bow. "I wanted to see my nephew, and I had some business to attend to in London."

Alisabeth held out her arms. "My turn, if ye please." She cooed and buried her nose against the child's neck.

Desire surged through Gideon as he watched her with the babe. Now that he had Lissie's affections, he wanted to plan a future—and a family. He knew she loved him. He did not know if she would give up Scotland for him.

"He's a bonny bairn, isn't he?" she asked, looking over her shoulder as he moved behind her.

He kissed the top of her head and inhaled her lavender scent and the infant's unique smell. "Yes, he's *verra bonny*," he answered in a terrible imitation that elicited moans from the family. His chest tightened when he imagined their child. A daughter with Lissie's glossy sable locks and his MacNaughton blue eyes. A son could come later.

"Well Stanfeld, are you up for a visit to White's tonight and lose a bit of blunt? Pendleton is in town and Lady Eliza will spend the evening here." Marlen gave Etta a kiss on the lips and winked. "I think we should leave the females to childbirth and baby talk. I've had my fill for the past month."

"That's a splendid idea, my love. Stay out as long as you like." She winked back at the viscount. "You have my permission."

***

Gideon relaxed into the soft leather armchair with a snifter of brandy. The oak paneling gleamed in the candle-light; muffled voices of patrons floated from the hall. He had walked away from the gaming table flush with funds, much to the dismay of his companions. For the first time, guilt riddled him. He would not gamble anymore. When he looked into another player's eyes, it was not good judge of character that told him if the man bluffed. No, it was that blasted legacy. His pride would not allow him to cut a sham, and his practical nature refused to throw money away on games of total chance.

"I wish I had your luck," Pendleton said again. "I tell you, I want to be there when you finally lose."

"Well, that'll be a long wait since I'm giving it up."

"Giving it up? Why, man? You're my hero at the tables." Marlen refilled the crystal glass, his gray eyes twinkling. "It's how we met, you know, Pendleton. I'd run out of brass playing whist. Gideon had a pile of winnings and a sister who was pining for a rake."

"I thought she set her cap for you, not the other way around," exclaimed Pendleton.

"I was only supposed to distract her from the rogue, which I did." He gave Gideon a side look and smirked. "I had no idea what I was getting into."

"All's well that ends well, as they say." Gideon grinned. "Tell me you're not a happy man."

"High in the ropes, my friend, high in the ropes." Marlen held his glass up. "In truth, I'm in your debt."

"Speaking of beautiful women, Stanfeld, when will you make an offer on the Scottish chit?" Pendleton grinned. "Was she really hiding in the heather?"

Gideon laughed, remembering their last conversation at White's. "No, Alisabeth was in plain sight. And I think I'll wait until we return to Scotland this summer."

"That's months away," scoffed Marlen. "I've seen you look at her. Why would you put yourself through that?"

"I want to be sure she'll accept England as her home. That's the only detail I can't predict. While my Lissie isn't fickle, she's a Highland lass through and through." He studied the intricate plaster moldings along the ceiling. "I'm luring her with my charm and good looks so she cannot imagine life without the Earl of Stanfeld."

"A few passionate kisses never hurt either," Pendleton said with a chuckle.

"Your position and wealth would be more than enough for most bird-witted females at Almack's," Marlen added. "There's something to be said for a woman who loves the man and not the title."

"A toast!" Pendleton emptied the decanter into their snifters. "To beautiful wise women who know our minds before we do. May we never be without them."

***

"I'm so happy you finally saw reason and allowed us to have this small dinner party." Lady Pendleton laid a hand on Lord Marlen's arm, her violet eyes twinkling. "Etta needed a distraction. That babe hiccups and she fears it's pneumonia."

"You are welcome, Eliza." Marlen smiled as he gazed across the room at his wife, her hands moving dramatically as she conversed with a group of guests. "When we found out Lachlan had been invited—and accepted—even Gideon agreed to stay a bit longer."

Alisabeth pressed her lips together to hide the smile. Sending a letter to Lachlan had been her idea. Knowing Gideon would want to get back to Stanfeld and oversee the spring planting, she'd needed a legitimate excuse to prolong the visit. Etta and Eliza had been so convincing in their need for a social event after Etta's long confinement. Never having sisters, Lissie had been easily caught up in the camaraderie between the two close friends. Besides, she and Etta may be sisters one day. The thought sent a hot rush through her.

"You're the most beautiful woman in this room," whispered Gideon from behind.

Her earlobe tickled from his warm breath. She closed her eyes, willing her body not to turn and fling itself against the delicious man hovering over. "And ye must be the most handsome earl in the room." His return chuckle made the tiny diamond drops at her ears tinkle. A Christmas gift from Maeve that Lissie guessed Gideon had purchased.

"I'd like to introduce you to some friends, if you don't mind," he said in a more proper tone. He held out his arm and they walked into the adjoining salon.

Lissie tried to still her racing pulse. What if these friends did not like her? Did not like Scots? What if—

"They'll love you, of course."

The words calmed her thudding heart. How did he know? How did he always know what ailed her? "Ye always know the right words, my lord. It's one of the things I've always admired about you."

He guffawed and his lips pulled into a titillating smirk. "The correct verbiage may come out of my mouth, but if you could hear the occasional jumble inside my head... Well, let's just say you would not be as impressed."

"Och, there is not much that could lower my opinion of ye, Lord Stanfeld. Or yer friends." She squeezed his arm. "I'm looking forward to meeting new acquaintances."

The first was an attractive older man with silver streaking his white-blond hair. "You've been holding out on us, Stanfeld. Who is this diamond of the first water?"

"Mrs. MacNaugton, may I present Sir Horace Franklin. He was a business associate and close friend of my father's since I can remember." Gideon inclined his head toward the older gentleman. "And this is my good friend Lord Sunderland."

Both men bowed and Alisabeth ducked in a slight curtsy, not sure if that was proper protocol or not. Gideon had not mentioned any titles, and she was still learning the intricacies of the *ton*.

"It's a pleasure to meet you," replied Sunderland, a gleam in his black eyes. "So this is the exquisite creature who bewitched Stanfeld."

She blushed. Maeve had warned her that rumors spread through London faster than a plague on a ship. "I'm afraid I canna take the credit. It was the faeries that bewitched him. I just happened to be the first female he laid eyes on after they cast their spell."

Both men laughed and Gideon smiled good-naturedly. "I suggest you keep her away from Grace. Your wife will have her and the faeries casting out the ghosts at Sunderland Castle."

"Ghosts?" That garnered Lissie's attention. "Your home is haunted?"

"By one of my ancestors, it seems. My dear wife has been pouring through books to find out how to send them on their way." Sunderland ran a hand through his raven hair. " In the meantime, she's managed to make friends with them. Or so she tells me."

"How do you make—"

"There ye are, lass. Ye're harder to track than a deer with wings." Lachlan's voice boomed from the doorway. "Come and give yer handsome brother a hug."

Alisabeth almost ran to Lachlan and threw her arms around him, squeezing him tightly. "How are ye, ye big brute? Any limp?"

"Nay, I could race ye around Hyde Park on the morrow." He looked around, his blue eyes sparkling with mischief at the stares they were receiving. "It appears affection is not shown between family at parties. Or perhaps in all of England?"

She giggled. "Perhaps not with the same enthusiasm as we Scots share. But I must say, ye are the best dressed man in the whole of London."

Lachlan patted his dress sporran, hung about his waist with a silver chain, and then pointed his toe to show off his polished black buckle shoes, fine tartan hose, and silver garter flashes. With a grin, he looked around the room. "I'll have to agree with ye, lass. I am indeed."

"When did you arrive? Did you settle in at the town-house?" Gideon asked as they shook hands. "I thought perhaps you ran into some bad weather."

"I arrived late last night and didna want to bother ye. I took a room at Limmer's and finished up some business this afternoon." He winked at Lissie. "Now I'm ready for some entertainment and a meal."

"You're in luck. It's almost time to eat." Gideon slapped his cousin on the back just as dinner was announced.

The guests began moving toward the door when Lissie heard Lachlan swear under his breath. Before she could ask what was wrong, he was striding across the room. His wife Fenella stood in the far corner, her eyes darting around the room as if looking for a way to escape.

"Did ye ken Lachlan's wife came with him?" she asked Gideon.

He squinted and took in the woman shaking her head at Lachlan. Angry tears shone in her eyes, and she shook her head violently, sending her white blonde curls flying against her wet cheeks. Then the Scott turned on his heel and marched from the room, fury reddening his face.

"What was that?" she asked as the woman ran through another door, escaping the curious eyes of the guests.

"I would venture to guess my son-in-law just discovered how disobedient his wife can be. She's with child now, and he didn't want her traveling," replied Sir Horace. "If you'll excuse me?"

"I never thought I would see the mighty Lachlan brought down by a female. He's certainly met his match." Gideon, an impish grin on his face, placed her hand in the crook of his elbow as the older gentleman followed his daughter from the room.

"This will set the London tongues wagging about your Scottish relatives," Lissie said with a laugh.

"Mama always said if you want to avoid humdrum, invite a MacNaughton."

CHAPTER THIRTEEN

"A hero is no braver than an ordinary man, but he is brave five minutes longer."

— RALPH WALDO EMERSON

Late March 1820
Stanfeld Estate

"*I* didn't want to interrupt your breakfast, my lady, but a letter arrived in the post for you." Sanders placed a silver tray in front of Lissie. "Since it was from Scotland, I thought you'd like to see it immediately."

She touched his arm as he drew away. "Thank ye, Sanders. Ye are so kind to me."

"Of course, my lady," he mumbled, red seeping into the deep crevices of his neck and cheeks.

"The only other person who has ever been able to make that man blush was my little sister, Helen," said Gideon with a shake of his head. "And it was her *lack* of manners rather than her sweet ways that caused it."

Alisabeth ran a knife under the wax. "Odd, it's a plain seal, not the Craigg's or MacNaughton's." She opened the paper and scanned to the bottom. Apprehension skittered up her spine. "It's from Colin."

"Why would he be writing to you?" Gideon put down his cup of coffee and leaned forward. "There must be something wrong."

Lissie read the words, her voice unsteady.

March 23, 1820

Madam,

If ye are still willing to help us, come to Glasgow. Merchants gather to demand representation, and skilled artisans cry for fair wages. The turmoil is creating mobs of angry, hungry folk with Lachlan in the thick of it. The political group he's involved with is talking rebellion, and I fear for him. A late blizzard hit the Highlands, so Calum canna come. I'm not in the position to advise the lad, but he'll listen to ye, his brother's widow.

Colin

"How old is that letter?" Maeve asked from the doorway, her face pale as ivory.

"About a week." Lissie stood, her brow furrowed with concern. "Maeve, you dinna look well."

Gideon was at her side, helping her to a chair. Lissie poured more tea, irritated with her unsteady hand.

Gideon saw her distress and took the cup, handing it to his mother. "Drink this, Mama. Did you not sleep well?"

"I had a dream, a terrible dream." Fear shone in her blue eyes. "It was a double hanging. I dinna know the first man but the second was Lachlan."

Lissie sank into the chair next to Maeve, her hand over her mouth. Peigi had told her about Maeve's visions. She did not doubt this one, though there was hesitation in Gideon's eyes. *Not Lachlan too. They canna take both grandsons,* her mind screamed.

"Let's not jump to any conclusions." The earl gritted his teeth.

"I must leave for Glasgow immediately," Lissie said in a raw voice, the panic rising in her throat. "I must pack."

"I will go with ye, lass." Maeve went to rise from the chair.

Gideon put a hand on his mother's shoulder. "You will do no such thing. I will go."

"Lachlan may not listen to ye, Gideon. If the English have anything to do with this, he could question your loyalty." Maeve's eyes were hard. "We must all go."

"I'm sorry but I cannot allow it. It's too dangerous." He bent and kissed the top of her head. "Have faith in me, Mama. I'll have Sanders begin preparations now."

Several hours later, Gideon pulled her into his arms. "I will see that no harm comes to Lachlan. Promise me you will look out for Mama."

Alisabeth nodded and he pressed his lips to hers. A soft, sweet kiss that made her long for a future and a family with him. She blinked back the tears. What if he could not save Lachlan, or Gideon was pulled into the fray? He nuzzled her neck and she breathed in his familiar scent of orange and spice.

"I love you, my sweet Lissie," he whispered in her ear, his warm breath tickling her skin.

She clutched his great coat. "Dinna go, Gideon." Throwing her arms around him, she kissed him back with a desperate passion. "I love ye with all my soul. My heart will wither away and die without ye."

He grinned, mounted Verity, and tipped his hat. "I'll see you soon, love."

Lissie watched him ride away until he was only a speck on the road. She walked back inside to a flurry of servants, and Maeve shouting orders over the commotion.

"What is happening?" Alisabeth watched the woman who had appeared pale as death a few hours before. "What are ye doing?"

"Packing, of course. I'm still the Countess of Stanfeld, lass, and my son willna be telling me what I can and canna do." She patted Lissie's cheek. "Now hurry, the carriage will be around soon."

***

April 1, 1820
  Glasgow, Scotland

A chill ran down Alisabeth's spine as the carriage moved along a busy Glasgow street. Tension hung in the air, groups of men gathered in front of taverns and spoke in low voices. Others paired off in alleys with furtive glances to the side, as if a threat might come from any direction. Danger permeated the air, and she gripped Maeve's hand. Signs were tacked up on street corners:

STRIKE IN SCOTLAND
BE HEARD ON 3 APRIL
A Committee for Forming a Provisional Government

. . .

"I dinna understand. Ian said he was part of a peaceful group. But these signs are demanding artisans to strike on Monday." She rubbed her temples. "It doesna make any sense."

"Gideon canna fight this. It's been brewing for too long. These men are making a stand, and I doubt the English will let it remain peaceful." Maeve peered out the window as they left the congested business area and entered the residential area. Their townhouse came into view. "It looks like Gideon went straight to the mill. Good, we'll change and do the same."

"He will be verra angry," Lissie said, almost smiling as she thought of the tick in his strong, handsome jaw when he was irritated. "Please let me take the blame for this. I dinna want him upset with ye."

"Nonsense. It was my idea and I take full responsibility." The footman opened the door and barely had time to put down the steps before Maeve issued orders and rushed inside, ignoring the shocked look of the servants. "Unload the baggage and place it in our rooms. We will be here at least a week so send for extra help. When our maids, tell them we need assistance straight away." With that she headed up the stairs.

Lissie gathered her skirts and tried to keep up. "Do we have a plan?"

"Of course. We'll go to the mill and speak with Colin." She grinned. "Once we have the details, we will speak with Gideon."

"And if we see Gideon first?" That awful knot was back in her stomach. "He'll turn us on our heels and send us right back to England."

"He'll have to carry *both* of us out if my intuition is correct about you. We've come this far, we canna stop now." She turned at the doorway of her chambers after shooing in the lady's maid. "We leave in ten minutes."

. . .

The entire city seemed poised on the edge of a precipice. If someone had lit a match, she was sure Glasgow would have exploded into bits. There were more signs posted by the Committee. Some had been torn down and ripped to pieces. Alisabeth shivered as they pulled up in front of the factory. Across the street, a figure hovered in the alley. Shadow hid his face but something about him seemed oddly familiar. With an uneasy certainty, she knew the man was watching their arrival.

"Not everyone is in favor of this strike," remarked Maeve. "There are too many hungry families who canna afford to lose a day's pay, let alone a husband's or father's income."

The coachman opened the door and handed the ladies onto the pavement. "You may return in an hour," Maeve ordered as they entered the gloomy stone building.

The familiar sounds and sights of the looms at first put Alisabeth at ease. When Colin appeared, his massive form blocking the office door, panic seized her. What if she could not help Lachlan? What if she let them all down? She swallowed the self-doubt and took a deep breath, setting her shoulders. Maeve was here to help. A voice whispered to her that this was her chance to honor Ian and make things right for her and Gideon. Retribution for her husband's death and atonement for loving another man.

"Lord Stanfeld said ye wouldna be coming." Relief eased the creases about his light blue eyes and mouth. "I mean no disrespect toward his lordship, but Lachlan is convinced this fanatical group has the right of it. They mean to strike across the country with force if opposed, and I dinna see the English taking kindly to it."

"My nephew is as pig-headed as his brother. He won't stand in the shadows and let others fight for him." Maeve walked past Colin and sat down in one of the mismatched chairs. "We must convince him there is a more imperative struggle right here."

Lissie gave the man a tight hug and plunked down on the hard wood, letting Maeve's words sink in. Yes, if Lachlan thought the mill was in jeopardy, he would remain here to protect it with his life. She blew out a breath as Maeve continued talking, a plan formulating as they each added their thoughts.

"The Committee called a meeting and Lachlan attended. Gideon has gone to find him. There are three new members that I dinna trust. They came looking for work a few months ago and made fast friends with Lachlan." Colin rubbed his jaw. "I told him not to bring the jackanapes to a meeting but he wouldna listen. They're rabble rousers, and I dinna ken which side of the fence they stand on. I'm afraid, come Monday, it will be a Peterloo Massacre all over again but more widespread."

A chill rippled over Lissie's skin. "I think someone is watching the building. Are the employees here joining the strike?"

"They've been told they willna be paid but willna be fired either unless they raise arms against us. It's up to them, whichever way their conscience decides." He grunted. "I've made it plain that it'll do more harm than good, with families going hungry and men most likely dying."

"I remember the uprising in Edingburgh when I was a girl," said Maeve, pain clouding her eyes. "A horde of men dinna see reason and will follow whoever leads them. The wrong man at the front will cause chaos. Remorse willna bring back lost lives."

The door slammed open, and Gideon's shadow fell across the desk. Lissie forced herself to breath and turned to face him. His jaw tensed, a muscle ticking along the edge. She was prepared for the anger in his steely blue eyes but concern also creased his brow. Regret stabbed at her heart to cause him such worry but knew there was no other choice.

"Dinna go yelling at Lissie," Maeve spoke, her hand up as if to hold off the explosion she thought was sure to come. "Once I've set my mind to something, ye canna change it. I admit it, I'm more obstinate than yer father."

The corner of his mouth turned up, but the hint of his bitter smile vanished when Lachlan came up behind him "The *appointment* was cancelled. My cousin has been filling me on the military training that some groups have been providing. He doesn't seem to understand that bearing arms against the government is treason. The penalty for treason is hanging. *Only* hanging, if you're lucky."

"I understand that wages for weavers and other skilled artisans were halved a dozen years ago. Petition after petition has not increased their earnings since." Lachlan's stormy blue eyes flashed with disgust. "This is one of the few factories with a decent wage, and that's only because Da insisted on it. Between the growing population of poor and constant cholera outbreaks, the people are being pushed into a rebellion."

Alisabeth stood. "Ian wouldna want ye giving yer life for a cause that canna be won through violence. If ye stand with them, ye'll die with them. I'm certain of it." She placed a hand on his arm, her eyes pleading. "Come back to the house and talk this out. We'll find a way without risking yer neck."

The angles of his face hardened, and Maeve stepped in. "Lachlan, we'd never tell ye to ignore yer principles. But I would ask that ye use the intelligence God gave ye and make sure ye are going about it the right way."

His shoulders relaxed slightly as he worked his jaw. "I'll come with ye but I'm not making any promises."

Colin let out a loud breath. "That's all we ask, mon."

Gideon escorted the women back to the carriage. "Is there some Scottish concoction we can put in his food tonight to make him see reason?"

Maeve laughed. "Now why would a Scot have a potion for that? We prefer to believe in the unexplained."

***

Gideon tied the cravat, cursed, loosened it, and retied it again with another curse. He could strangle Lissie and Mama for being here. The two most important women in his life trapped in a country on the edge of revolt. If he hadn't seen the Truth in those scoundrels' flitting gazes, he'd pick both females up, throw them over his shoulder, and drag them home. Instead, he had to tell Lachlan that he'd looked into the eyes of three men in that tavern and spied treachery. Not heard a plot, or discovered a note, or found anything that would be real proof. Only that he'd *seen* it in the depths of their perfidious souls. He yanked on the waistcoat with a grunt of annoyance. He'd find the words. He had no choice.

In the drawing room, his cousin lounged on the burgundy velvet settee, his head lolled back against the intricate green and gold embroidery framing the cushion. He looked exhausted. His mother stood near the fireplace, the dancing flames showing dark shadows against her pale face and highlighting the streaks of silver in her auburn hair. He joined her and leaned against the mantel, accepting a glass of claret from a servant.

Alisabeth entered, a delicate gray muslin gown swaying against her shapely legs. Her smile maddened him and stirred his blood at the same time. He wanted to scoop her up, carry her up the stairs, and make love to her until she screamed with pleasure. God's bones, he wanted this over so he could concentrate on making her his wife. He dismissed the servant and closed the door.

"Aunt Maeve was telling me about her dream. I admit it

causes me more than a bit of alarm." Lachlan began as soon as they were alone. "I want ye to know I dinna take it lightly."

Gideon snorted. "I've made that mistake myself."

Lissie settled next to Lachlan. "Colin is worried also. He thinks there are spies working within the weavers."

"Three of them." Gideon pushed away from the fireplace and paced. "They were at the tavern but not sitting together. They've had pamphlets printed and will distribute them over the next few days, inciting Scots to take up arms."

"Which three men?" asked Colin, alert and following Gideon intently as he wore a path in the Axminster carpet.

He shook his head impatiently. "I don't know their names."

"But ye could recognize their faces? Their voices?"

"Their faces yes, not their voices. I didn't hear a conversation." Gideon tensed, waiting for the reaction sure to come.

"Then how in the bloody—"

"I saw the Truth in their eyes." He yelled back at Lachlan. "It sounds insane, but I know without a doubt those men are not who they say they are. If you continue on your course, you will hang as a traitor."

Alisabeth picked up her brother-in-law's hand and held it between both of hers. "Lachlan, it's true. He saw it in Ross Craigg's eyes. Calum recognized the gift, and he'd tell ye to heed this warning."

Lachlan narrowed his eyes at Maeve. "Aunt? I'm sure ye have an opinion. Ye dinna come all this way to sit in silence."

She shook her head with a sad smile. "Ye ken how I feel. I've told ye my dream."

He leaned on his knees and scrubbed his face with his hands. "Gideon, would ye come with me tomorrow afternoon? Since the assembly was dispersed, we set up a time to meet above a bookstore. I can try to dissuade some of them from joining the military drills, and maybe ye'll recognize the three turncoats."

Gideon breathed a sigh of relief. One catastrophe avoided. He prayed they had changed the course of Mama's dream. "Yes, if you think I can help, I'm willing to accompany you. With the understanding that *no one* leaves this house." He glared at Mama then Lissie. "We don't need anything else to worry about. Is that understood?"

Alisabeth nodded solemnly. His mother grinned.

***

Gideon had left earlier that afternoon. Alisabeth leaned back on the chair, one leg propped over the armrest, her foot twitching restlessly. She couldn't keep her mind on the book in her hand. Maeve looked up from her needlepoint when the butler entered the drawing room.

"My lady, a note has arrived."

"Could they be done already?" Maeve tore open the envelope, unfolded the paper, and skimmed it quickly. "Please order the carriage right away."

"But Gideon said—"

"This is from Lachlan. We're to meet them at the mill." She rose and smoothed her dress. "Let's find out what our men have accomplished, shall we?"

Less than an hour later, the women entered the mill. Lissie recognized two of the older children who toted water buckets. She smiled at them and they bobbed to her with shy grins. When the ladies entered the office, Colin looked surprised.

"To what do I owe the pleasure, ladies?" He stood and met them at the doorway. "Lachlan and his lordship didna mention yer visit."

"We received a note from Lachlan to meet us here."

Colin scratched his head. "What did it say, exactly?"

Lissie's chest tightened as she turned to Maeve. Something was wrong. Very wrong.

"It only said to meet him here and he'd explain. It looked as if it had been scrawled quickly. I assumed…"

Colin smiled reassuringly. "I'm sure it's fine, Maeve. Please be seated and I'll be right back."

Alisabeth took a deep breath and wiped her sweaty palms against her skirt. She pushed down the panic that rose in her throat. The anxiety must have shown in her eyes.

"I think we've been duped. But why?" Maeve drummed her fingers on the wooden armrest. "Did they want us out of the townhouse or here in particular?"

Raised voices echoed from the hall. A bell began to clang. Lissie and Maeve ran into the large workroom and saw the employees running to the front of the building. Lissie sniffed. *Smoke!*

Colin barreled down the aisle. "The storeroom is in flames. Out with ye, now!" He pushed them behind the other employees. Fenella, Lachlan's wife, shoved through the escaping crowd and tried to push past Colin. "No, lass. Ye're going the wrong way."

"I need to go upstairs and make sure the women heard the bell. I'll meet you on the street." She disappeared, only her white-blonde hair visible as she made her way down the smoke-filled hall.

A crowd had gathered at the entrance, and the shrieks of panic grew steadily louder. They were not moving.

A crowd had gathered at the entrance, and the shrieks of panic grew steadily louder. They were not moving.

"The door is blocked," someone shouted, "we're trapped."

Colin jumped on top of a loom. "This way!" He waved and pointed to another door. Jumping off the machine, he ran to the heavy steel door and pushed. It didn't budge.

Maeve gripped Lissie's hand. "Stay calm, lass, and we'll find a way."

She nodded and watched as Colin picked up a bucket and threw it at the window. The glass shattered and formed a jagged opening. He slammed the thick pane with another bucket until he created a hole big enough for a person. Yanking material from several looms, he threw the cloth over the serrated glass and climbed out.

Cries of terror followed him and another man scrambled on top of the machine to peer out the window. He cupped his hands around his mouth and shouted, "MacNaughton's coming back. He's got ladders."

A bleeding Colin clambered back over the sharp edges of the windowsill.

"Up ye go!" Colin yelled to a young girl of twelve or thirteen.

He lifted the girl up as if she were a bag of cotton, and she disappeared over the uneven windowpane. The other man followed Colin's lead, dropping a woman onto the second ladder. The workers pushed and shoved toward the safety. The smoke increased, billowing through the hall and into the workspace.

Lissie's eyes watered, and she covered her nose to reduce the amount of smoke going into her lungs. "Maeve," she called through the shawl, "you have to get out of here."

"This is our mill and we're responsible for these people. I'll not leave before the women and children are out." Maeve found a large box and set it in front of the loom. She stood on top, keeping two orderly lines for evacuation on either side. Her commanding voice seemed to calm the workers and the press of bodies eased.

A frantic young woman called two names over and over. "Mary, Frances. Oh lord, oh lord. Mary! Frances!"

"Is someone missing?" Lissie called to her over the din. "They may be outside already."

The girl shook her head. "They haul carts back and forth to the store room. My wee brother and sister."

Lissie's legs went weak. "How old?"

"Seven and ten."

Alisabeth picked up her skirt and pulled the shawl from her shoulders. "I'll find them. Go and wait outside!" Running toward the storeroom, she saw Fenella return with a dozen women, their faces streaked with smoke and tears, hacking and coughing but alive.

Fenella grabbed her. "Where are you going?"

"Two little ones are back there. Mary and Frances."

"Sweet Jesu! I'll get more help."

Alisabeth stumbled down the hall, tears streaming from her eyes. The heat increased with each step. Getting down on her hands and knees, she called for the children. There was a little more visibility at this level, and she stopped at an open door. The room was dark but she called their names. As she backed out of the doorway, Lissie thought she heard a whimper. "Mary! Frances!" A racking cough.

The crackle and snap of burning timber echoed in her ears. Flames licked at the ceiling above, creeping toward them like a predatory wolf. She crawled into the room, feeling her way until her fingers touched a foot. A small hand grabbed her arm, tiny nails digging into her skin. "I've got you! What's yer name?"

The girl squeezed Alisabeth around the neck, sobbing and coughing. "M-m-mary."

"Where is Frances?" The girl pointed.

The boy was lying on the ground, not moving. Saints and sinners! Her fingers grasped his collar and she pulled then crawled. Pulled then crawled. Mary clung to her. Blood ran down Lissie's neck from the girl's imbedded fingernails. She made it to the hall, pulled the shawl from her head, and placed it over Mary's face.

Sizzling flames danced above her, searing her skin. The smell of burnt hair permeated her nose and blocked her air passages. She tried to breathe through her mouth but gulped in more smoke. Mary's wheezing turned into short, desperate gasps. Without the shawl over her head, her lungs struggled to pull in air. The heat singed her throat. *Keep calm, keep moving.* Crawl, pull. Crawl, pull. Crawl... Her muscles wouldn't obey her mind any longer. Winded and weeping, Lissie covered the children with her body before the blackness consumed her. *I'm so sorry, Gideon. So verra sorry...*

CHAPTER FOURTEEN

"The nose of a mob is its imagination. By this, at any time, it can quietly be led."

— EDGAR ALLEN POE

The smoke spiraled into swollen gray clouds above the skyline. Gideon peered in the direction of the fire. "That's close to the mill."

Lachlan studied the sky then picked up the reins and slapped the horses. "Hiya!" The animals lunged forward, sending pedestrians scattering. "It *is* the mill."

By the time they reached the river, the block was crowded with employees who had escaped the burning building, family members looking for loved ones, and rows of bucket brigades on either side of the mill. Wooden buckets and leather bags were dipped into the Clyde and handed down the line. As water splashed onto the stone and the flames shot out of the far end of the factory, Lachlan shook his head. "Spittin' in the wind."

Gideon grabbed a boy by his arm. "What happened?"

"The mill caught fire and the workers were trapped inside, my lord."

"What?" He shook the lad by the arms. "Is everyone out?"

"Don't know for sure, but the supervisor got most of 'em out a window. Some of 'em went 'round and opened the door but it took a while. The bolt was broken in the lock."

Gideon squinted from the smoke and spotted a man talking with Lachlan. The weaver from the tavern. The spy. He called to Lachlan, who nodded his head as the man talked, waving his arms.

"He says he stopped a mon with an English accent running from the fire. He knocked John down in his haste to get away." Lachlan turned back to the weaver. "Thank ye for yer help, John."

The man nodded and tried to move on but Gideon pulled him up by the collar and stared into his eyes. Gideon heard the slam of a bolt in his head but did not see flames in the man's eyes. An accomplice. "You locked them in, you bloody bastard."

The man squirmed and fought to get away. "Take yer hands off me!"

"Gideon, we must find Colin."

Lachlan, not understanding why Gideon detained the man, pulled hard on his arm. The conspirator twisted from Gideon's grasp, hit the pavement, and scuttled away.

They pushed through the throng toward the front door. "Have ye seen Colin?" Lachlan yelled to a group of men. They pointed to the other end of the building. They found Colin, standing inside a shattered window, smoke still pouring out above his head. His face was smeared with ash and his hands wrapped in a ragged black cloth, staunching the blood that dripped down his forearms. He deposited an equally filthy woman onto the ladder. Mama.

Gideon rushed forward just in time to scoop her up in his arms as she stumbled to the ground. "Mama, what the hell are you doing here?"

She hugged him, her raspy voice faint in his ear, "Lissie went after two little ones." She coughed and gasped. "In the store room."

A sledge hammer pounded his chest. Colin appeared next to him and he handed his mother to the giant. "I'm going after Lissie. Which way is the fastest?"

"Take the ladder," he yelled. "I'm right behind ye."

Gideon looked over his shoulder and saw Lachlan now holding the countess. *What in God's name were they doing here? I'll thrash Lissie if we both get out of this alive,* he thought grimly, dread gutting him like a pig on a spit.

A hand caught his elbow. He turned and accepted the wet wool blanket Colin slammed into his chest. He motioned for Gideon to follow him, and they made their way toward the hallway that led to the storeroom. He was glad to have the supervisor's bulky form in front of him because it was impossible to see anything until you stumbled into it. His feet seemed to be made of lead as the smoke engulfed them. He had heard scraps of conversation in the crowd. The fire had been contained to one end of the mill. If Lissie was outside the storeroom, there was still a chance.

He put a hand out blindly, his fingers finding and latching onto Colin's coat. His eyes watered and the smell of charred wood stung his nostrils. His throat burned with the effort of swallowing. Colin stopped abruptly. Gideon's nose smashed into his back then the man squatted to the floor. Gideon took another step and his foot made contact with something. Crouching low, he felt a limp hand.

"Get Lissie, I'll carry the wee ones," came Colin's muffled voice as he rolled her lifeless body off the children.

Gideon's stomach lurched. He fumbled along her unmoving form, found her head then her legs, and scooped her up into his arms.

"Ready?"

Gideon nodded and followed Colin back out. His eyes burned and he swore, not able to see Lissie's face. The smoke thinned, and the broken window came into view. Gideon began to run, coughing and sputtering as prayers he thought he'd forgotten came to his lips. *Don't die on me, love, don't die.* He kissed her gritty face as men climbed the ladder and took her from him. He scrambled down after them.

A crowd gathered around Colin, a mother wailing, a child coughing then vomiting. He knelt beside his sweet Lissie, held her hand, and kissed her lids. "Wake up, love. Wake up." He lifted her head, removed the damp wool blanket, and wiped her face. Looking up, he searched the sea of faces for his mother. She would know what to do. Lachlan appeared in the throng, his arm around Mama. Behind them a familiar face bobbed in and out of the crowd. Gideon blinked and wiped his eyes with one hand, trying to focus.

Ross Craigg.

"Colin! Colin!" The supervisor turned at the hoarse shout and followed Gideon's finger as he pointed. Recognition lit up the Scot's red-rimmed eyes, and he nodded then disappeared. Craigg realized he'd been seen and turned tail.

A grating moan brought Gideon's attention back to Alisabeth. Her eyes fluttered open, puffy and the most beautiful red he'd ever seen. A wave of relief washed over him and he lost his balance, falling back on his bum and drawing the first deep breath since entering the building. His body rocked with a spasm of painful coughs. Maeve plopped down next to him, placed a cold cloth on Lissie's forehead and handed one to him.

"Och, lass. Ye scared me so," she said as she wiped Lissie's face.

"The children?" she croaked then gagged, rolling to her side.

Maeve smoothed the hair from the girl's cheek as she expelled bile from her throat. Her eyes watered, her nose ran, and Gideon thought she'd never looked more beautiful. A cup of water appeared in Maeve's hand, and she offered it to Lissie once she stopped coughing.

"The children are alive, thank the heavens." Tears streaked the older woman's face and her voice caught. "I'd like to give ye a thrashing, but I'd have done the same thing."

"Can you breathe now?"

She nodded. "If I dinna breathe too deeply." The sentence caused another torment of coughs.

Gideon gently lifted her onto his lap and rocked her back and forth, knowing he'd never let her go again. "Good God, I thought my life had ended when we found you unconscious. You're never leaving my sight again." He buried his head in her neck. The faint smell of lavender mixed with smoke reminded him how precious life could be. "No more heroics, do you understand?"

She nodded, gave him a weak smile, and closed her eyes.

"We've got him. He admitted to taking payment from English moles to start the fire." Lachlan's harsh voice cut into his thoughts. "He's on the docks with Colin, surrounded by a mob. A verra angry mob."

"I can't leave her and Mama. You take care of it." Gideon eyes did not leave Alisabeth's face.

"Son, our carriage is on the way, and I've sent for the physician to attend us at the townhouse." She laid a hand on his arm, and he saw the coldness in his mother's usually warm eyes. "Go and tend to business now."

Lissie's battered face from the previous encounter with Craigg flashed in his mind. "Yes, you're right, Mama. I believe a reckoning is at hand."

"Do not let laws and righteousness keep ye from doing what's right. That man needs to pay for what he's done." His mother patted his shoulder and kissed him on the cheek. A familiar coachman appeared, helped her to her feet, and then gathered the sleeping Alisabeth in his arms. The threesome made their way through the thinning crowd.

Lachlan held out a hand. Gideon grasped his cousin's wrist and pulled himself upright. As they neared the dock, he spotted Craigg's sneering face and rage filled him. His heart slammed against his chest; his fists curled and uncurled. He could kill the man himself. They shouldered their way through the jeering men, workers employed by MacNaughton Textile. The hair prickled on the back of his neck. They wanted blood as badly as he did himself.

Colin had found a length of rope and tied Ross' hands behind his back. When Gideon stopped in front of the bound man, he spit at Gideon's boots.

"I'd think you'd be more cooperative, considering the circumstances," Lachlan said, and then punched the man in the nose. Blood spurted out, speckling the front of Gideon's shirt and mixing with the soot and dirt. The men jeered and shouted.

"Just one question," asked Gideon. "Why?"

"I should have been chieftain of the Craiggs. When that whore's father married her to a MacNaughton, it created *peace* between the clans. *Peace*"—he spit out the word, saliva and blood clinging to his own boots now—"and I prefer power. Then ye came with yer witch's ways, and I had to sacrifice my daughter because the high and mighty MacNaughton declared it."

"You were willing to murder all these innocent people to get revenge?"

"I'd have sold my soul to the devil. When the English spy offered to pay me to set the fire, it only sweetened the pot." The man's eyes held such intense fury, Gideon knew there was no hope for him.

Colin yanked his head back. "*Ye* sent the note, ye sniveling snake."

"Just figuring that out, are ye?" Ross laughed, a mocking sound that grated on Gideon's nerves. "My special thank ye to that whore of yers for shooting at her own kin."

Reform was impossible for such an addled mind. "Where are the authorities? I want this mongrel out of my sight."

"Weel, the constable and I have an understanding. He'll be back in an hour. If Craigg's still here, he'll be jailed and put on trial." Colin raised his voice. "What say ye? Do we leave him to the courts?"

"My boyo was in there with me!" came a shout.

"He could have taken out my entire family!" cried another.

"We'll take care of him!"

"Hangin' is too good for him."

Craigg struggled against his constraints. "I ken my rights. I'll have a trial, ye cowardly devils."

"Ye'd murder innocent women and children and call us cowards?" A man near the front yelled and threw a rock, hitting Craigg in the chest.

Gideon rubbed the back of his neck and looked back at the Scot, watching the vehemence. Fear had replaced the malicious satisfaction in his eyes.

"No. Wait, no. Dinna let them have me. They'll tear me to pieces." Ross fell to his knees, his voice now a pitiful whine, his lips trembling. "Please, I'll take my chances with a hanging."

"Ye seem to have plenty of courage when ye're smacking around a woman or have a paid brigand to back ye up. Ye're a sorry excuse for a Scot and a man." Lachlan grabbed the hair on top of the traitor's head and jerked the man to his feet. "Cousin, it's time we check on the women. We'll leave this pig to his fate."

Colin shrugged his shoulders. "I feel a mighty thirst coming on and dinna think I want to wait an hour for the constable." He gripped Ross on the shoulder. "Stay here and wait for him like a good lad, eh?"

Gideon steeled himself as the three left the dock. Ross' shrieks were drowned out as the mob surged forward. He did not look back.

CHAPTER FIFTEEN

"I have drunken deep of joy, And I will taste no other wine tonight."

— PERCY BYSSHE SHELLEY

April 5, 1820
Glasgow, Scotland

*L*issie nestled into the feather mattress and rested against Gideon's hard chest, listening to his heart beat as he dozed. Her body was slowly mending, but the physician insisted a full two weeks before they attempted any travel. Her lungs would need time to heal. Exertion of any kind could cause shortness of breath so the trip to Stanfeld Manor would be much too taxing. Exercise would need to be introduced slowly into her daily routine, he had warned.

Lissie wouldn't argue. The first few days had been a haze of voices and prompts to swallow the liquids forced down her throat. A dark form, smelling of orange and spice, had murmured sweet words of comfort and love. Gideon. The earl, according to Maeve, had never left her side. The fatigue showed in the shadows beneath his deep blue eyes. Even now, he stretched out beside her on top of the counterpane, his boots gleaming in the candlelight. She snuggled deeper, the slick material of his waist coat cool against her cheek. He stirred, his lips brushing the top of her head.

"Awake, my sweet?"

His breath ruffled her hair, and she nodded, eyes closed, comfortable in the warmth of his embrace. When she'd tried to talk yesterday, she'd sounded like a bullfrog. Gideon had barked a laugh, which had made her giggle. That had caused such pain in her throat, tears sprung to her eyes. The poor man had looked as if she'd dealt him a physical blow. Nothing more than a whisper, Maeve had suggested, until she was able to speak without pain. Or Gideon was far enough away not to see or hear her distress.

A soft knock at the door and the countess entered. "The maid is bringing up a broth for supper. Perhaps tomorrow, if ye're feeling stronger, I could have a chess board set up." She bent over her son and kissed Alisabeth on the cheek. "The color is returning to yer cheeks."

Lissie smiled and pushed herself up against the pillows. She should be embarrassed to have a man lying next to her, clad only in her nightdress. At least it was her favorite one, made of soft rose linen and gold scallops at the neck and sleeves. Maeve had scoffed at the physician's mention of proprieties, so Lissie decided to enjoy his closeness.

"Once we're home, I have no doubt Sanders will see to every detail of her recuperation." He stretched and untangled his arm from around her body. "Did Lachlan bring any news?"

"He said he'll bring us up to date at breakfast tomorrow. Most of the strikes have been quelled, and the newspaper didna report any new disturbances. According to the butler, more English regiments arrived this morning." She sat down in a chair beside the bed. "It's surprising there havena been more fatalities."

"Once the leaders are rounded up, the trials will begin." Gideon shook his head. "I wonder if it would have come to this if those blasted spies had not stirred up the skilled artisans and factory workers."

"We'll never ken for sure," Maeve's voice was heavy with regret. "Perhaps something good shall come of it. It isna only the Scots merchants unhappy with Parliament."

Lissie sipped her broth and dozed. When she woke, Gideon was slumped in the chair next to her bed. A glass of brandy sat precariously in his hand. She leaned over to remove it from his grasp, but his other hand shot up and held her wrist. He leaned down, brushed his lips against the soft skin of her forearm, and made a trail of fiery kisses to her palm.

"You've already stolen my heart. Will you take my nightcap as well?"

"I prefer yer heart," she whispered.

"You have it." He stood and swirled the golden liquid. "The question is, do I have yours?"

With a smile, she nodded and held out her arms. He set down the brandy, slid onto the bed, and pulled her close. His breath was hot and tickled the sensitive skin below her ear, sending goosebumps down her arms. His lips brushed each eyelid, her nose, the corners of her mouth. His tongue traced the line between her bottom and top lip. She sighed and opened them, letting him explore her mouth and tasting him in return. The brandy was sweet with a hint of citrus. Or was that him? Her mind was muddled with passion. It didn't matter. She whimpered when he ended the kiss, burning her tender throat.

"Sweetheart, I had planned to wait until our trip to MacNaughton Castle but with the events of the last few days..." He brushed a stray tendril behind her ear and traced the curve of her neck with his finger. She shivered. "Will you marry me?"

Maeve's words echoed in her head. *Can ye imagine yer life without him?* She pushed a glossy black lock off his forehead and cupped his cheek. "Yes," she whispered.

***

July 1820
Stanfeld Manor

"If Mama packs anything else, we'll need to add another wagon." He lowered his voice. "I'm surprised she's not taking Sanders along."

"He refused. Be patient with her. She's arranged the perfect wedding and doesna want to forget anything. There are the gifts for the villagers that she promised on the last visit. And the wooden horse for Nessie and Hamish's bairn, bolts of cloth for Peige and Glynis." Alisabeth counted the items on her fingers. "The train on my wedding dress is long enough to take up an entire trunk."

They walked in the garden, enjoying their last night before leaving for Scotland. Gideon had suggested, much to the delight of his betrothed, being married at MacNaughton Castle. His sisters would arrive by the end of the month, and the wedding would be held in early August. Lachlan and Fenella would attend, along with Colin and his betrothed, and they would meet once more in Glasgow on their way back.

The Lowland city had quieted. Trials had been held in Glasgow and Stirling for the radicals and several had been sentenced to hang, while more would be transferred to penal colonies in South Wales and Tasmania. Eventually the lords would have to listen to the merchants and allow them a voice in Parliament. And the merchants, in turn, needed to improve working conditions and increase wages. But for now, there would only be a single hanging in Glasgow, not a double.

He stopped and pulled Lissie against him, her soft curves fitting against his hard length. A few more weeks and she would be his wife. The image of her on their wedding night made him rigid with desire. He dipped his head and pressed his lips to hers, breathing in her scent, feeling her long lashes brush against his skin.

"When I think of how close I came to losing you," he murmured in her ear. "It's like a knife to my heart."

"Maeve said something the other day about the attraction of opposites. She and Charles were so different, as we are, yet we fit together perfectly." She leaned into him, and nipped his bottom lip. "It made me think of our time in Glasgow. The unrest helped us realize how much we meant to each other. Two contrary passions brought us together."

"Rhapsody and rebellion," he murmured, kissing her again with all the hunger of a man who'd found what he wanted and would never let go.

***

Reviews are the life blood of an author. If you enjoyed this story, please consider leaving a few words about Rhapsody and Rebellion.

Read Book #4 in the Once Upon a Widow Series

Earl of Darby

A MacNaughton Castle Romance is my steamy series published by Dragonblade Publishing in 2020. Book #1 will begin with Lachlan and Fenella's story. You can find it the links here on my website.

HISTORICAL NOTE

There were multiple riots in England and Scotland from the late 18th century through the time of our hero, Gideon, Earl of Stanfeld. This story includes three of them. The main characters and their actions are fiction. The backdrop of the rebellions is not. Below is a brief summary of the rebellions featured in this book.

The King's Birthday Riots were protests against the 1791 Corn Laws. (The Corn Laws were tariffs on imported food and grains. Meant to keep grain prices high and benefit British mercantilism, they instead magnified the already poor economic situation due to bad harvests and war.) The riots lasted for three days in Edinburgh and coincided with the birthday of King George III. One person was killed, many injured, and an effigy of the Lord Advocate, Dundas, was hung and burned.

The Peterloo Massacre occurred on August 16, 1819. Sixty to eighty thousand people gathered to hear the radical orator, Henry Hunt, speak at St. Peter's Field in Manchester. His message advocated for political reform and repeal of the Corn Laws.

The local magistrate was nervous about such a large gathering and sent the yeomanry to arrest Henry Hunt. They charged into the crowd and trampled a woman and her child. Disorder erupted and the 15th Hussars were sent in to disperse the crowd. In the end, 15 died and 400-700 injured. The name Peterloo Massacre derived from the earlier Battle of Waterloo.

The Radical War, or the Scottish Insurrection of 1820, occurred in central Scotland. A week of strikes and conflicts, aimed at Parliamentary reform, was organized by factory workers and skilled artisans, a majority of them weavers. It was later discovered that government agents (English and Scottish) infiltrated the close-knit organization of weavers. Deaths, injuries, and arrests of the organizers were the final result.

The English government feared a revolution similar to France, so the agents purposefully agitated unrest to expose the radical leaders. Across Scotland, 88 men were eventually charged with treason. In Glasgow, James Wilson was accused of "compassing to levy war against the King in order to compel him to change his measures." He was hung and then beheaded on July 20, 1820. It is said that he climbed the scaffold, looked out at the crowd, and said to his executioner, "Did ye ever see sic a crowd, Thomas?"

Andrew Hardie and John Baird were hanged and beheaded in Stirling in August. Almost twenty men were sentenced to transport to New South Wales or Tasmania.

Maeve was correct, however, and something did come from the tragedy. Electoral reform did not end with the rebellion. The Scottish Reform Act of 1832 significantly changed voting in Scotland. The Scottish electorate increased from 5,000 to 65,000, adding the voices of the general population to the few elite.

Sign up for my newsletter and don't miss any new releases.

https://www.subscribepage.com/k3f1z

EARL OF DARBY

HER INNOCENCE AND CANDOR REVIVED
THE CHIVALRY BURIED DEEP IN HIS SOUL.

Prologue

There is a fountain fill'd with blood
Drawn from Emmanuel's veins;
And sinners, plung'd beneath that flood,
Lose all their guilty stains.

— "PRAISE FOR THE FOUNTAIN
OPENED", OLNEY HYMNS, 1779

Mayfair, London
December 24, 1814

"I must admit, Mama, you were right." Nicholas tugged at his cravat, snowy white against the dark blue of his waistcoat. "She is a diamond of the first water."

"Of course she is. The betrothal benefits both families. Lady Henning and I will have beautiful grandchildren, and you will not lose your inheritance. I will never forgive your father for his recklessness, gambling away such a sum." Lady

Darby's expression hardened as she spoke of her husband, but her tone was that of a doting mother. "You are the most handsome viscount in London. What an earl you will make one day."

"Let's not wish Father away too soon. It was not *all* his fault." Nicholas took a final look at his own reflection, a mirror image of his mother's that peered back at him. They had the same burnished-gold hair and clear, light blue eyes. But the lines around her mouth had deepened, and more worry lines creased her forehead. Their gazes held for a moment and then she busied herself, brushing imaginary specks from the back of his waistcoat.

"The Duke of Colvin cheated. Granted, Father should never have staked so much on a hand of cards, but the man is a blaggard. And his son is no better, perhaps worse if the on-dits are true."

"Yes," she muttered, still avoiding his eyes. "I've heard the same. Now, it's your wedding day, and we should speak of happier times to come."

"Agreed, it's been a trying year, but I believe the darkness is behind us now." His father, the Earl of Darby, had lost an enormous amount to the blackhearted nobleman. It had been a night that still haunted his dreams. Colvin's taunting, the slow anger that had built in the earl, the vicious smug smile when that extra ace had been laid on the table. Nicholas knew the man had cheated but could not prove it. One didn't accuse a duke without proof. Even then, it would have been dangerous.

They'd had to sell most of their property to settle the debt of honor and avoid scandal, barely holding on to the estate. The debacle had taken a toll on his father's health. "You seem to have come to the rescue, Mama."

"Nonsense. Lady Henning wanted her daughter to move up in rank. As a baron's wife, this is quite a feather in their cap. Alice will be a countess when you assume the title. And we needed the dowry."

"And the lady was willing?"

"You asked her yourself, did you not?" His mother studied the evergreen garland that decorated the hearth mantel, fingering the sprigs of rosemary and ivy leaves. "What woman would not be happy for such a match? Handsome, titled husbands are hard to come by."

"I beg to disagree. *Penniless* titled husbands are more easily found, handsome or otherwise." He smirked at his mother's pursed mouth.

"I could not ask for a better Christmas celebration than having a new daughter enjoying our Yule log. I realize the banns were read rather hastily, but our family shall begin a new chapter with the New Year." She smiled up at him, her blonde hair gleaming in the sunlight that slanted through the gauzy curtains. On tiptoes, she kissed his cheek. "I must go. We leave for the church within the hour."

As Nicholas watched her leave, the image of his own children playing in front of the Yule log crossed his mind. He wanted children. Several, at least. Would they be dark like Alice or fair like himself? His stomach inexplicably tightened at the thought, and he attributed the discomfort to the approaching wedding and loss of bachelorhood.

Nicholas and his best friend from university, Gideon, the future Earl of Stanfeld, stood before St. George's, Hanover Square. The giant columns towered over them as they stood on the steps of the church. Complete opposites in looks and temperament, they had made quite a name for themselves during their time at Cambridge.

"So, did Lady Darby attach the leg shackles or was this of your own making?" Gideon grinned, his black hair shining in the morning light, deep-blue eyes twinkling with laughter.

"Though I admit Miss Alice would tempt the staunchest of bachelors."

"Let's just say I don't mind making the sacrifice. And with any luck, it might turn into a love match." Nick adjusted his cravat for the tenth time since leaving the manor. "Is Pendleton coming?"

"He'll be here." Gideon slapped his friend on the back. Viscount Pendleton was the third member of their infamous university trio. "Nervous?"

"I wouldn't call it that, more a sense of foreboding." He shook his head. "I've been listening to Sarah and her fairy-tales too much of late. The Grimm Brothers have her mesmerized."

"Your sister doesn't need anything to spark her imagination." Gideon reached inside his coat and pulled out a flask. "A flash of lightning to steady the hand?"

"Gladly accepted, my friend."

***

"Calm yourself, Alice. I didn't mean to raise my voice." Nick smoothed back her rumpled dark hair, tipping up her chin. Deep shadows below those shimmering coffee eyes made her pale skin almost glow. She was magnificent, ebony upon ivory, docile and pliant. Or had been until he realized she'd been taken before their wedding night. While consummating their union, he found there was no barrier within her to breach.

"I was just surprised you weren't a…"

"A v-virgin."

"There is someone else? You've already given your heart to another?" A first love, an infatuation perhaps that would fade in time. He was confident in his own looks and love-making skills to overcome the attempts of a clumsy boy.

She sniffed and shook her head, raven waves bouncing against her bare shoulders. "I can't continue this charade any longer. I am so sorry, so so sorry."

"I beg your pardon?" An icy finger of dread skittered down his spine.

She lifted a tear-stained face to him. "I am with child."

He froze, the muscles of his face paralyzed. His mouth hung open, but no words would emerge. Heat washed over him as her perfidious words sunk in. Trying to pull his thoughts together, he tied his shirtfront closed. *Hell and damnation...*

An annulment. He would get an annulment.

"I was forced."

"Raped?" He blew out a breath and ran his fingers through his hair. Had she led on a previous suitor? A flirtation gone badly? This was not how his wedding night was supposed to play out. "Who is he?"

"A nobleman's son. Mama said it would be his word against mine, that he would never be brought to justice, but I would be ruined." She grabbed his arm as he tried to stand. "Please, our mothers came up with the idea. I was against it, but I was pregnant. I—"

"Thought it would be easy enough to pass the whoreson off as my child. I was in need of funds, and you were in need of a husband." The spark of anger ignited, flames burning his stomach. What an imbecile he'd been. "Whose bloody child am I expected to raise in order to keep my estate?"

"Mama said it must be kept secret. He must never know. He's a vicious, despicable man. We don't know what he would do." Her eyes went wide with fear, those full lips he'd just kissed, trembled. "Please, don't make me tell you."

"By God, you will." Nicholas grabbed her narrow shoulders, pressing into the smooth skin, his fingertips creating red imprints in the creamy flesh. "I'll know whose by-blow I have beneath my roof."

Alice began to sob in earnest, her chest heaving as she tried to breathe, her fingers clenching his hands. "I am so sorry. So sorry..." Her head moved back and forth as she muttered her apology over and over.

He wrenched free and stormed across the room to open the window sash. He needed air; he couldn't breathe. Pressing his head against the upper windowpane, he looked out onto the dark landscape and let the chilly breeze cool the angry fire consuming him.

Alice let out a low wail, a sickening moan of pain and anguish, and clutched her belly, sinking to the floor on her knees. The light from the fire highlighted her wet cheeks and cast long, incongruous shadows off her small, delicate form. "Forgive me, please. Forgive me."

"Forgive you?" His hand curled into a fist, and he punched the wall, needles of pain searing from his knuckles through his wrist. "I am betrayed by my own mother, then my wife *on my wedding night.*" He laughed, the sound ugly and grating. "I believe I've reached my limit of absolution."

His entire body went taut as a wire. He had to get out, away from her tears, away from this hoax of a marriage. He'd been used. Nick pushed away her clinging hands as he dressed, barely registering the crimson smear his bloody knuckle left on the sleeve of her night rail.

"Don't leave me. Please, I'll make it up to you. I'll do anything," she whispered, her voice tinged with panic. "Where are you going?"

"Away. Anyplace I won't have to look at another conniving female." He yanked on his boots and threw open the door. "When I return tomorrow, we will sit down with both our *dear* mothers. By Christ, I will learn the truth."

Storming down the stairs, he bit out orders to the

footman to bring round his carriage. "No, have my horse saddled instead." He needed to get away. He needed to get drunk. He needed to wipe this nightmare out of his mind.

Nicholas rode out of town, his mind whirling, cold sweat dripping down his back, his face hot with temper. Women. If his own mother betrayed him like this, how could he ever trust another female? He thought of his sister, her innocent face, and wondered if she would also grow duplicitous with age.

As he entered the outskirts of town, he squeezed his gelding's sides, sending Arthur into an easy canter and breathing in the chilly night air. The stars were bright in the black sky and twinkled merrily, mocking his mood. No snow tonight.

With a sharp kick, they galloped on, white puffy clouds trailing behind them as Nicholas left his wife and that horrid scene behind. The pounding of hooves seemed to beat in the same rhythm as the curse echoing through his mind. *Bloody hell! Bloody hell! Bloody hell!* By the time the horse tired, his anger had eased. Calmer and more rational, he turned his mount around and headed back toward the lights and noise of London.

Yes, Alice had deceived him, but she'd been as much a victim of their mothers' scheming as he had been. The poor girl had been raped, packaged off to a convenient husband, and never had the chance to look for love or even affection. Never had a say in the matter. At least he'd had a choice.

It would take time to adjust to the fact she was with child. But they had consummated the marriage, and he needed her dowry. Without it, his family would be on the rocks. His pride had been dented when he'd seen himself as hanging on Alice's sleeve, the arrangement too one-sided for his liking. But now it seemed they were even; they were using each other. So be it.

He'd deal with his mother later. For now, he'd go home to

his *wife* and tell her they would come to an agreement and move on with their lives. He'd pray to God she had a girl. There was no way he would acknowledge a bastard as his heir.

Nick arrived back at the terrace house, a sleepy groom waiting on the steps to take the reins. "He needs a good cooling down. I rode him hard."

He took the stairs two at a time and threw open the door to his rooms, his chest heaving with the effort of the ride and two long flights of stairs. "Alice…" It was cold. Had the servants let the fire die?

In the sitting room of their apartment, a note lay on the table next to the door. He collected it from the silver tray, recognizing his name written in flowing letters.

Nicholas

With the envelope in hand, he entered the bedchamber. "Alice—"

An invisible iron bar hit him full force. He stumbled toward the bed, his body teetering before he sank to his knees, the letter drifting to the carpet. His eyes never left the petite body swaying from the upper rail of the four-poster bed.

Her white gown fluttered from the light breeze of the still-open window. Delicate satin slippers swung lazily before his eyes. Slowly, his gaze rose past the hand wearing his emerald wedding ring, the limp arms, to the vacant eyes of his dead wife. Her head tilted at an awkward angle, her delicate chin resting against the linen sheet tied around her long, slender neck. The once-porcelain skin he'd stroked and kissed a few hours ago, now mottled and gray.

"NOOOOOOO…" Nicholas clutched his head, rocking back and forth, cursing his wife, his mother, himself. He rose, clutched the bedcurtain, and climbed onto the mattress. Face-to-face with his dead wife, his heart clenched, the breath gone out of him. Nicholas tenderly pushed a damp tendril from her cheek. The coldness of her skin against his scraped knuckles jarred him, and he frantically began to untangle his wife from the bedclothes.

Tears blurred his vision; he cursed his trembling fingers as he tried to maintain his balance on the mattress. Finally releasing her from the linen noose, he fell to his knees and cradled her in his arms, swaying gently side to side. The door opened, and he heard a terrified gasp. He looked into his mother's horrified eyes.

"What have we done?" he whispered. "What have we done?"

Chapter One

"...In as much as every discovery of what is false leads us to seek earnestly after what is true, and every fresh experience points out some form of error which we shall afterwards carefully avoid."

— JOHN KEATS

Wicked Earls' Club, London
Late October 1819

"It's just a friendly game of whist. C'mon, Darby, play with us." The marquess made another unsuccessful attempt to bring Nicholas into the game.

"I beg your pardon, my lord, but I don't indulge in gaming." Nicholas, Earl of Darby, shook his head, an easy smile curling his lips. His gaze swept the crowded room. Several men sat to his left near the fireplace, sipping drinks and engaged in conversation. Flanking the right side of the room were tables where various games of whist, faro, and hazard were in progress. "A friendly wager in the books, whether the heir will be born or a ninth daughter, perhaps whether Stanfeld will marry before he's sixty, is as far as I go."

"I'm in the books?" Gideon, the Earl of Stanfeld, scowled, his bushy dark brows coming together. "How in tarnation did I get in the books?"

"Once a man inherits an earldom, he becomes much more interesting." Nicholas laughed and slapped him on the back. "Just an example, my friend. You are not a line in the club's wagers." He chuckled. "Yet."

"I think I already regret putting you up as a member in the Earls' Club." Stanfeld tapped the golden *W* pinned to his friend's lapel. "Your standing improved, and I don't see you any closer to the parson's trap than I am."

A faded but familiar pain grazed Darby's heart, and he forced another grin. "I escaped that snare once, if you remember." He stopped a man in livery passing by. "Bring us a bottle of brandy, would you? We'll be in the billiard room." He nodded to Stanfeld and took his escape.

Nicholas made his way down the stairs, his thumb rubbing against the *W*. Wicked. Yes, he was a wicked earl and planned on keeping that title and this pin for many years. His vices did not hurt anyone nor interfere with his title or family.

Stanfeld had recommended him to the elite club. He'd had the requisite qualifications—trusted among his peers and claimed the title of earl and bachelor. The benefits included an exclusive floor of this club, a set of private rooms for each, and almost any vice for the asking. He had utilized the reserved rooms frequently. In fact, this had become a second home ever since the death of his father, a week after Nicholas's ill-fated marriage.

He had built up his reputation as a rake over the past several years, the gossips helping tremendously after his wife's death. According to the on-dits, the Earl of Darby had drowned his sorrows in alcohol when his wife had mysteriously died. Some said she had been so frightened of his wedding night demands that she had killed herself. Others spoke in whispers of possible murder, only wanting the poor chit's money and knowing that, as a peer, he could get away with it.

Neither family had ever commented or spoken of the night, much to the dismay of the prattlers who wanted the sordid details. It had taken years to quiet the tongues. But the rumors still kept nosy mothers at arm's length, worried for their innocent daughters. It kept him off the list of suitable bachelors.

In reality, the suicide had been dealt with quietly, with all the efficiency that a peer-related catastrophe was always handled. The law requiring the forfeiture of a suicide's property—in this case, dowry—was circumvented with a verdict *of non compos mentis*. A jury of his peers determined that Alice had not been of sound mind when she'd committed the deed. Alice's mother had testified to her daughter's melancholia the days before and of the wedding.

Nicholas rolled his shoulders, the expensive coat hugging his frame, and shoved that unpleasant memory away. Instead, he concentrated on the delightful redhead that would be waiting for him later in his rooms, after a mind-numbing bottle of brandy and a few games of billiards with his two closest friends. He would never repeat the mistake of his father, having no appetite for gaming. His poisons of choice were drink and the type of woman with no desire for a husband.

His present liaison was a prime article who had the misfortune to be a married to an elderly baron. The husband went to bed early in the evening, and she stayed in Nicholas's bed until early morning. They'd been meeting weekly for the past year, and it was a pleasant arrangement for both. With the confidentiality afforded by the Wicked Earls' establishment, however, his mistress could easily be whisked in and out of his rooms at the club, and no one would be the wiser. Though at times, he felt a twinge of pity for the aging baron.

Nathaniel, Viscount Pendleton, sat in a highbacked leather chair near the fire, legs crossed, head back, a glass in his hand. The embers glinted off the silver cufflink of his sleeve as he swirled an amber liquid against the cut crystal. His brown hair still held streaks of gold from the summer sun, and his green eyes were thoughtful.

"How did the brandy arrive before me? I just ordered it." Nicholas stopped at the side table and poured himself a drink from the decanter. "You seem pensive."

"I ordered a bottle of my own. I know how you hate to share, Darby," said Pendleton with a smirk. "And yes, I'm pondering a dilemma."

He sat down next to his friend, sinking into the soft leather and crossing his polished Hessians at the ankles. "Let's wait for Stanfeld, and you can tell us both at once."

"Tell me what?" The Earl of Stanfeld entered the room, followed by a man with a bottle. "Thank you, Edward." He took the decanter and set it next to the one already half-empty.

"I have a problem," said Pendleton.

Stanfeld's brows rose as he poured a drink. "A monstrous one, if the amount of alcohol is any measure."

"Ha! Nothing better than three muddled heads coming up with a solution. I'm sure we could take care of mine and solve all the world's problems with just one more bottle."

"No, that would take at least four." Nicholas stood, tossed back his last swallow, and poured another. The pleasant warmth was spreading through his body, a promise of sweet numbness and a night of dreamless sleep. He picked up a billiard stick and moved it from one hand to another, checking its weight, its straightness. "Who is the first challenger?"

Pendleton shook his head. "I'll yield to Stanfeld. You both play, and I'll talk."

As the men began their game, Pendleton told his story. "You know my sister, Hannah, was supposed to have her first season last year."

Both men murmured agreement, then with a nod from Nicholas, Stanfeld hit the first ball with a loud *crack.*

"Yes, she changed her mind about a season in London when you married Lady Eliza. Decided to get to know her new sister and wait until she was eighteen." Nicholas grinned at his opponent's miss, bent, and sent a ball into a corner pocket. "Hoping to find some sweet, handsome landowner close to home, we assumed."

Pendleton nodded. "Well, she didn't find one and was to come out this winter, arriving in Town after Eliza had the baby in late December or January. But now, Parliament has called a special session in November due to the Peterloo Massacre."

Nicholas studied the table and his next move before looking up. "Nasty business, that. Poor souls meeting at a peaceful assembly to hear a speaker, then slaughtered by their own skittish local government."

"By the by, Stanfeld, I am sorry about your cousin's death in that fiasco. I do hope your mother has recovered sufficiently?" Pendleton laid a hand on his friend's shoulder. "Bloody bad luck, that was."

Stanfeld's mouth tightened, and he nodded. "Thank you,

and yes, she's doing well. His death brought about a long-postponed trip to Scotland to see Mama's ancestral home." His countenance brightened. "I almost gave in and wore a demmed kilt but knew I'd only get tangled up in the deuced thing. Now, about the Special Session. You aren't in the House of Commons, so how does it affect you?"

"It doesn't, but *you* are both members of Parliament and will be in Town..." Pendleton paused, looking uncomfortable. "Hannah wants to come for the *start* of the season. I could accompany her here, but I can't leave Eliza alone for too long."

"You *won't* leave her alone, you mean," quipped Nicholas. It was well known that Pendleton was a bit overprotective of his wife. She had been abused by a malicious father, who had tried to kidnap her while under the viscount's protection. The father had made a fatal mistake crossing Pendleton. "I haven't seen Hannah since she was a child. What kind of woman has she grown into?"

"I need you to protect her, not ogle her," said Pendleton. "Both of you."

"Won't your mother accompany her? She'd be protection enough from roving eyes." Nicholas had met the dowager viscountess once during a summer party at Pendle Place. She had been a formidable woman. Her icy stare could freeze a man in his tracks. "Anyway, I'm happy to be of assistance since my sister is also coming out."

"Thank you. My mother still hates coming to Town and is using the arrival of her first grandchild to avoid it." Pendleton sighed.

Stanfeld laughed. "Believe me, her daughter can be just as daunting. Hannah's a bit too assertive for my taste, but she's a tempting armful."

"She'd love to hear the tempting part." Pendleton held his glass up to Stanfeld. "You know she still sets her cap for you.

I think she's convinced once you see her in London, dressed and mingling with the *ton*, you will fall at her feet and beg her forgiveness for not noticing her remarkable beauty sooner. You could even act as if you don't recognize her."

Stanfeld spit his drink out and swiped at his splattered cravat. "Good God, man, it would be like bedding my sister, and I refuse to encourage her. I, uh, have my eyes on someone."

"Oh? Did you find that bonny lass hiding in the heather while you were in Scotland?" Pendleton teased, remembering a conversation they'd had the previous summer.

The earl turned red. "As a matter of fact, I did. Mama liked Lissie so much, she brought the chit back with us. As company for her this winter, so she says."

"So she says," Pendleton and Nicholas echoed.

"Back to your dilemma. So, you want us to keep an inconspicuous eye on your sister, I assume. I'm happy to accommodate when I'm here." Stanfeld paused and took a sip of his brandy. "However, I will only attend the more pressing sessions until February. My sister is also expecting, so my mother will insist on a long visit then. Otherwise, I'll be spending more time in the country."

"So we get to meet this Scottish lass?"

Stanfeld looked embarrassed. "Truthfully, she is my cousin's widow."

"And here I thought Darby was the only scoundrel among us."

"It's not like that," Stanfeld added quickly. "They were betrothed from birth and had more of a friendship than passionate love. She's unlike any woman I've known, except Mama."

"I've heard those Scottish lasses are lively," Nicholas teased. "I look forward to meeting her."

"Back to you, Pendleton. Who will be chaperoning

Hannah if not your mother?" Another *crack,* a missed shot, and a mumbled curse from Stanfeld.

"It seems Aunt Bertie has volunteered."

This time, Nicholas coughed and spluttered. Lady Roberta was infamous in her appreciation for the male physique. Almack's had refused her entrance for a time. "I'll never forget that tabby's chubby fingers pinching my backside."

Stanfeld guffawed, mischief in his black eyes. "I heard you took the lady up on her overture."

"Devil it, I doubt I could have kept up with her, even at the tender age of twenty. I thought she finally retired to the country."

"Well, she has offered her services and is my first line of defense against the randy bachelors. You, my friends, are the cavalry she will call in if needed."

***

Darby climbed into the waiting hackney with his leather satchel. The driver clicked to the mare, and she pulled away with a snort, proceeding toward the outskirts of Mayfair. It was after midnight, and his man would be waiting at the Guinea.

It was a small tavern, frequented by the staff of the wealthy. Grooms and footmen relaxed at the end of a long week and complained about their masters, telling secrets about the titled families who paid their wages. He opened the canvas bag and pulled out the homespun brown jacket, frayed neckcloth, and worn boots. Removing his hat and cravat, he leaned back against the worn leather squabs and pulled off his Hessians, donning the drab attire. A few blocks from his destination, he rapped on the roof and his driver stopped. He paid the man and, with a quick word and nod, arranged for the hackney to wait.

"I should be back within the hour," Darby said as he handed him a pouch of jingling coins. He'd been using the same driver for the past year. They had come to an understanding. The hackney escorted him and kept mum; the earl paid a week's wages for a night's work.

"Aye, my lord, at yer service," the old man replied, pulling his hat down over his eyes and leaning back. "I'll be waitin' right here."

Walking the rest of the way, Darby's heels clicked along the slick cobblestones of the narrow street as he made his way toward the rendezvous point. Fog crept close to the ground, curling about his boots, obscuring the pavement, then slithering away to reveal a puddle or dark outline of something he instinctively knew to sidestep. A cold mist sent a chill through him. It shrouded the buildings, lending the streets a Gothic quality that had Nicholas picking up his pace.

We're getting closer, Alice. Your death will not be in vain.

He thought of the letter, the worn paper with the fateful words she'd left him that night. Even in her turmoil, she'd known her mother was wrong. The evil that possessed the Duke of Colvin must be stopped. And so, she had told him the name of the perpetrator in her final farewell.

He stopped in front of the Guinea, the light spilling out onto the wet stones and illuminating two dark forms around the side of the building. Their heads were close as if in secret conversation, and a small parcel passed between them. One of the men glanced up, caught Nicholas's eye, and scurried down the alley. One of Colvin's men. Good, that's why he was here.

He entered the noisy tavern, the scent of sweat, stale beer, and cheap perfume assailing his nose. A barmaid smiled at him over her tray. He avoided her gaze and quickly moved to a back table where Walters sat with a bumper of ale. A fire blazed in a large hearth along one wall, patrons crowded around it, sharing gossip.

Some were dressed in fine clothes, displaying their prominence in a household. Others wore homespun garb, workers from the area who cleaned the streets, made deliveries to the kitchens, or performed the city's necessary menial labor. An occasional bark of laughter or shout of anger could be heard over the steady thrum of voices.

"Good evening, my lord," greeted his man with a nod as he stood. Walters waved his mug at the maid, who nodded in understanding. "Seems the duke is moving up in the world of vices."

"I saw one of his toadies outside," Darby said, sitting down at the wood table, carefully balancing himself on the wobbly stool. "Looked as if he were paying for a service."

"Indeed, sir. We'll be heading over to the Rat's Nest as soon as yer ready." His ruddy face wore a smile that didn't quite meet his brown eyes. Walters had been a Bow Street runner before working for the earl. He'd been wrongly accused of bribery when he'd come too close to solving a crime that involved a nobleman and still held a grudge toward certain aristocrats.

"St. Giles? The gin houses of Covent Garden aren't keeping him satisfied now?" Darby accepted the mug and took a long pull. "Where in this delightful rookery are we destined?"

"Seems there's an interesting purchase at one of the flash houses." Walters ran thick stubby fingers through his tangled dark brown curls, tipped with premature gray. "A house that specializes in procuring chimney sweeps."

"But Colvin isn't looking for a boy to sweep his chimney."

Darby's lip curled in disgust. "Is that the transaction I witnessed outside?"

"I would assume it is." Walters winked at the barmaid as she plunked down another bumper. "Thank you, lass."

"It seems the old duke kept his son's depravity in check while he was alive. In the past year, he's gone from gambling and elegant prostitutes to gin houses. The type known for catering to hard-to-please clients." Darby drummed his fingers on the glass and took a long pull of his ale. "He's succumbing to his dark side."

"The question is, how far will he sink? The abbess of the last place he patronized refused him entrance last week. Seems he's getting more violent and not worth the risk."

Nicholas had been watching the Duke of Colvin for the last year. A year of spies, of waiting for something that could be used against him. When Colvin's father had been alive, His Grace had kept a tight rein on his son. The previous duke had known what his heir was about and hired a bodyguard of sorts to accompany his undisciplined son. Keep him out of trouble.

Trouble. That's what the old duke had called Alice's fatal circumstances. *A troubling situation.* To date, Nicholas had witnessed several women unknowingly saved from Alice's fate as the expensive attendant had pulled his ward from a compromising scene.

In Darby's eyes, the bloody bastard *and* his father had been equally responsible for their part in Alice's death. And then there was his own role in the whole mess. So Darby, stricken with remorse, had made a vow. He would get justice for the woman who would never know love or a family of her own.

Patience. The man had been untouchable when his father had been alive. But now he was on his own, no restraining hand, not a soul to tell the wretch "no." In the past year,

Colvin had lost interest in the well-born virgins. He'd gone to the gin houses instead—those known to provide for clients with *peculiar* tastes—and enjoyed some rough sport with those working women desperate enough for the coin. But his lust for inflicting pain seemed unquenchable.

Darby tossed down a shilling for the unfinished ale and stood. "Let us venture into the Rat's Nest. I have a hackney meeting us a few blocks away."

"Aye, sir. I'm in the mood to catch me a repugnant little rodent."

ABOUT THE AUTHOR

USA Today Bestselling author Aubrey Wynne resides in the Midwest with her husband, dogs, horses, mule, and barn cats. Obsessions include wine, history, travel, trail riding, and all things Christmas. Her Chicago Christmas and Regency series have received multiple awards and nominated numerous times as a Rone finalist by InD'tale Magazine.

Aubrey's first love is medieval romance but after dipping her toe in the Regency period in 2018 with the *Wicked Earls' Club,* she was smitten. This inspired her spin-off series *Once Upon a Widow*. In 2020, she launched the Scottish Regency series *A MacNaughton Castle Romance* with Dragonblade Novels. Her Regency detective series, *Paddy's Peelers*, will launch early 2024.

Website: http://www.aubreywynne.com

Newsletter: http://www.subscribepage.com/k3f1z5

Facebook Group: https://www.facebook.com/groups/AubreyWynnesEverAfters/

MORE HISTORICAL ROMANCE BY AUBREY WYNNE

Once Upon a Widow series

Earl of Sunderland #1

Maggie award, International Digital Awards finalist

Grace Beaumont has seen what love can do to a woman. Her mother sacrificed her life to produce the coveted son and heir. A devastated father and newborn brother force her to take on the role of Lady Boldon at the age of fifteen. But Grace finds solace in the freedom and power of her new status.

Christopher Roker made a name for himself in the military. The rigor and pragmatism of the army suits him. When a tragic accident heaves Kit into a role he never wanted or expected, his world collides with another type of duty. Returning to England and his newfound responsibilities, the Wicked Earls' Club becomes a refuge from the glitter and malice of London society but cannot ease his emptiness.

Needing an escape from his late brother's memory and reputation, Kit visits the family estate for the summer. Lady Grace, a beauty visiting from a neighboring estate, becomes a welcome distraction. When the chance to return to the military becomes a valid possibility, the earl finds himself wavering between his old life and the lure of an exceptional—and unwilling—woman.

A Wicked Earl's Widow #2

Recommended by InD'tale Magazine

Eliza is forced into marriage with no idea her life will change for the better. Married less than a year, her unwilling rake of a husband is surprisingly kind to her—until his sudden death. The widowed Countess of Sunderland remains under her in-laws' protection to raise her newborn daughter. But her abusive father is on the brink of financial ruin and has plans for another wedding.

Nathaniel, Viscount of Pendleton, gains his title at the age of twelve. His kindly but shrewd estate manager becomes father and mentor, instilling in the boy an astute sense of responsibility and compassion for his tenants. Fifteen years later, his family urges him to visit London and seek a wife. The ideal doesn't appeal to him, but his sense of duty tells him it is the next logical step.

Lord Pendleton stumbles upon Eliza on the road, defending an elderly woman against ruffians. After rescuing the exquisite damsel in distress, he finds himself smitten. But Nate soon realizes he must discover the dark secrets of her past to truly save the woman he loves.

Rhapsody and Rebellion #3

Maggie finalist, nominated for Rone Award, InD'tale Magazine

A Scottish legacy... A political rebellion... Two hearts destined to meet...

Raised in his father's image, the Earl of Stanfeld is practical and disciplined. There are no gray lines interrupting the Gideon's black and white world. Until his mother has a dream and begs to return to her Highland home.

Alisabeth was betrothed from the cradle. At seventeen, she marries her best friend and finds happiness if not passion. In less than a year, a political rebellion makes her a widow. The handsome English earl arrives a month later and rouses her desire and a terrible guilt.

Crossing the border into Scotland, Gideon finds his predictable world turned upside down. Folklore, legend, and political unrest intertwine with an unexpected attraction to a feisty Highland beauty. When the earl learns of an English plot to stir the Scots into rebellion, he must choose his country or save the clan and the woman who stirs his soul.

Earl of Darby #4

Holt Medallion Winner, NTRWA Reader's Choice Award, Nominated for Rone Award, InD'tale magazine

Miss Hannah Pendleton is nursing her pride after her childhood crush falls in love with another. Determined to break a few hearts of her own, she hurls herself into the exciting and hectic schedule of a first season. Always clever and direct, the smooth manners and practiced words of the gallant but meticulous bachelors do nothing to stir her soul until…

Since his wife's suicide on their wedding night, the Earl of Darby has carefully cultivated his rakish reputation. It keeps overprotective mamas at bay and provides him with unlimited clandestine affairs. But when Nicholas sees a lovely newcomer being courted by the devil himself, her innocence and candor revive the chivalry buried deep in his soul. The ice around Nicholas's heart cracks as he desperately tries to save Hannah and right a hideous wrong committed so long ago.

Earl of Brecken #5

A seductive Welsh earl on the brink of ruin. A wealthy cit in search of a hero.

Miss Evelina Franklin reads too many romance novels. She's certain a handsome duke—or dashing highwayman—is in her future. In the meantime, Evie entertains herself with the admirers vying for her fortune.

The Earl of Brecken needs cash. His late father left their Welsh estate in ruin, and his mother will not let him rest until it is restored to its former glory. Notorious for his seductive charm, he searches the ballrooms for a wealthy heiress. His choices are dismal until he meets Miss Franklin. Guileless and gorgeous with an enormous dowry, she seems the answer to his prayers. Until his conscience makes an unexpected appearance.

A MacNaughton Castle Romance series

Highland Regencies

"Witty and sensual!"

Verified Purchase Review

"Lovely characters and complicated family conflicts. You will easily get caught up in their lives."

A Merry MacNaughton Mishap (Prequel)

Rone finalist, InD'tale Magazine, N.N. Light Book Heaven finalist

Two feuding clans, one accidental encounter, a wee bit of holiday enchantment...

Peigi Craigg has tended to her family without complaint since her mother's death. But now they ask too much. The English landlord has offered her uncle, the Craigg chieftain, an escape from debt and starvation. The price: Peigi must become the earl's mistress. If she refuses, the remainder of their clan must leave the Highlands. If she agrees, her hope of a husband and family of her own are lost.

Calum MacNaughton rescues a man from an icy drowning, only to find he's a member of the rival Craigg clan. The man swears to repay Calum for saving his life and broaches the possibility of peace between the clans. Months later, the Craigg reappears with his most precious possession, hoping to settle his debt before the new year.

Now Calum has until Twelfth Night to convince her to stay.

Deception and Desire #1

Nominated for Rone award, InD'tale Magazine, N.N. Light Book Heaven award winner

Two rebellious souls... An innocent deception... One scorching catastrophe...

Fenella Franklin is too tall, too intelligent, and has no title. Her talents lie in numbers and a keen business mind, not in the art of flirtation. When she becomes the object of a cruel wager during her come-out in London, she vows to put off the penniless noblemen vying for her sizeable dowry. But her season is cut short after her mother discovers the subterfuge, and Fenella retreats to Scotland.

Lachlan MacNaughton has neither the temperament nor the patience to be the next MacNaughton chief, preferring to knock heads together rather than placate bickering clansmen. He readily accepts a reprieve to help with the family's textile mill in Glasgow. A sizzling chance encounter in the rain introduces him to the new *female* bookkeeper. His grandfather may want him back in the Highlands, but his heart has been lost in the Lowlands.

The attraction between Fenella and Lachlan sparks a passion not even two rebellious souls can deny. But an innocent deception tests their newfound love and threatens the freedom they both crave.

Allusive Love #2

A woman in love... An infuriating Scot... A tantalizing chase.

Kirstine MacDunn has loved Brodie MacNaughton forever. He returns her affection—as his best friend and confidante. After enduring one too many of his infatuations, she finally takes matters into her own hands.

Brodie knows it is his destiny to lead Clan MacNaughton, but his grandfather insists the honor goes to the oldest. When Brodie and his brothers struggle to convince the chief that tradition is not always the best path, he turns to Kirsty for support. She surprises him with more than advice. A kiss that sends unexpected fire through his veins.

Pride, Highland politics, and tragedy collide, proving Brodie's ability to lead. But when a resentful clan member's revenge threatens Kirsty, he realizes how precious and allusive true love can be.

The Count's Castaway

The Count's Castaway is a bit of swashbuckling adventure rolled into a romance. A brave heroine, a suave wanderlust hero, a ship on the high seas and unexpected love all blend together to make this a must-read.

N.N. Light's Book Heaven

He's escaping his past... She's running toward her future... The present just got interesting.

Torn from her bed and indentured to an American as a child, Katherine Wilken demands her freedom seven years later. Denied her liberty, she stows away on The Escape, hoping to return to England. But when the ship sets sail, so does her heart. Katie soon realizes she's once again a captive—of love.

Narrow escapes seem to be Count Alexandre Lecroix's lot in life. Fleeing France as a boy during the Reign of Terror, he's a man with no country and soon takes to the sea in search of his destiny. The Napoleonic Wars have filled his pockets and his zeal for excitement, but his heart remains hollow. When he discovers a feisty stowaway on board, he resists the squall of emotion she stirs within him.

Two lonely souls find passion in the turbulent waters of the Atlantic, each a fugitive of their past. As land draws near, Zander is torn between his desire for a woman and his hunger for the sea.

Can love survive once the ship has anchored, or will their newfound happiness founder?

A Medieval Encounter Series

Rolf's Quest

Great Expectations winner, Fire & Ice, Maggie finalist

"Romance, destiny, family values & betrayal all played parts in this intriguing novel that had me turning each page in anticipation."

The BookTweeter

"I enjoyed the flow of the story and the sweet, charming romance. There were unexpected twists and turns that kept my pages turning until the very last page! I highly recommend taking a read through Aubrey's tapestry of Merlin, magic, and true love."

Verified Purchase Review

A wizard, a curse, a fated love...

When Rolf finally discovers the woman who can end the curse that has plagued his family for centuries, she is already betrothed. Time is running out for the royal wizard of King Henry II. If he cannot find true love without the use of sorcery, the magic will die for future generations.

Melissa is intrigued by the mystical, handsome man who haunts her by night and tempts her by day. His bizarre tale of Merlin, enchantments, and finding genuine love has her questioning his sanity and her heart.

From the moment Melissa stepped from his dreams and into his arms, Rolf knew she was his destiny. Now, he will battle against time, a powerful duke, and call on the gods to save her.

Saving Grace (A Small Town Romance)

Contemporary and Colonial America

Holt and Maggie finalist

This unique piece has the reader traveling between the early 1700s and the early 2000s with ease and amazement. The audience truly feels sorrow for Grace and Chloe and is able to connect with each woman for the hardships they are overcoming... The attention to historical facts and details leave one breathless, especially upon learning the people from the past did exist and the memorial erected still stands.

InD'tale Magazine

"I am becoming a pretty decent fan of the author I would say at this point. She managed in such a short amount of pages to thrill me with some lore, romance, and suspense."

Verified Purchase Review

A tortured soul meets a shattered heart...

Chloe Hicks' life consisted of an egocentric ex-husband, a pile of bills, and an equine business in foreclosure until a fire destroys the stable and her beloved ranch horse. What little hope she has left is smashed after the marshal suspects arson. She escapes the accusing eyes of her hometown, but not the memories and melancholy.

Jackson Hahn, Virginia Beach's local historian, has his eyes on the mysterious new woman in town. When she enters his office, he is struck by her haunting beauty and the raw pain in her eyes. Her descriptions of the odd events happening in her bungalow pique his curiosity.

The sexy historian distracts Chloe with the legend of a woman wrongly accused of witchcraft. She is drawn to the story and the similarities of events that plagued their lives. Perhaps the past can help heal the present. But danger lurks in the shadows...